★

Lying on the ground was a corpse.

He was facedown and the back of his head was a crusty mess of blackened blood. Between his shoulder blades, his tan cotton shirt was crunchy with the same substance. The desert was already working on the body, drying it out, turning it leathery.

I had the urge to run, but I fought it, knowing that Hellstrom, the Marlboro Man, watched.

Bracing myself, I waved away the swarming flies and squatted. I grabbed the corpse's heavy shoulder and lifted it slightly to get a look at his face. The bullets hadn't penetrated here, but scavengers had been at his eyes and nose and lips, leaving black holes where his features should've been. His mouth was pulled back in a maniacal grin. Red ants crawled around his eye sockets. I felt my breakfast rising, and I tried to leap up, but it was too late.

I vomited in David Field's face.

★

"A promising series."

— *Booklist*

Forthcoming from Worldwide Mystery by
STEVE BREWER

DIRTY POOL
CRAZY LOVE

shaky
GROUND

STEVE BREWER

W**O**RLDWIDE®

TORONTO • NEW YORK • LONDON
AMSTERDAM • PARIS • SYDNEY • HAMBURG
STOCKHOLM • ATHENS • TOKYO • MILAN
MADRID • WARSAW • BUDAPEST • AUCKLAND

SHAKY GROUND

A Worldwide Mystery/April 2003

First published by St. Martin's Press, Incorporated.

ISBN 0-373-26454-2

Printed in U.S.A.

To Max, Seth and Kelly,
in inadequate exchange for the time it took.
Thanks, also, to Frank Zoretich, Rich Henshaw
and all the folks at St. Martin's Press.

ONE

DON'T TRY TO FIND New Mexico on those national weather maps on TV. The weathermen always plant their big butts in front of us and the other rectangular Rocky Mountain states. They know where their viewers are, and it ain't out here. New Mexico has fewer residents than Philadelphia. Since about a third of them live in Albuquerque, a whole lot of the fifth-largest state is unpopulated. Sante Fe's trendy and Albuquerque's booming, but most of New Mexico remains a Big Empty.

I occupied myself with these thoughts to keep my mind off my airsickness. I was being thrown about in a helicopter as it zipped back and forth forty feet above the high mesa west of Albuquerque. We'd been at it for an hour and, so far, had seen one ranch pickup kicking up dust along a dirt road. There was no other sign of humans, just rolling land furred with yellow grass and dotted with blue sage and the occasional dwarf juniper. All the sameness made the dry riverbed known as the Rio Puerco a welcome squiggle whenever we crossed over its eroded banks.

The pilot, a lipless crag of a man named Reed Hellstrom, seemed oblivious to monotony. He casually guided the helicopter through its paces, scanning the ground from behind mirrored sunglasses. We wore headphones and microphones for communicating over the *wump-wump* of the chopping blades, but he'd said almost nothing since we took to the air. The padded headphones made me sweat. Whenever Hellstrom turned my way, I could see myself reflected in his sunglasses: my forehead glossy with perspiration, my hair flying around, my face tinged a distinct green from the back-and-forth motion of the aircraft. Bubba Mabry, fearless private eye, man of action, queasy copilot.

Hellstrom had outlined the search pattern for me before we left the blessed ground. Lift off from the Double Eagle Airport on the windswept mesa, then zigzag between the Rio Puerco and the mesa, eventually reaching the boomtown of Rio Rancho to the north.

"It's the same pattern we used in Nam, looking for downed pilots," Hellstrom had said, his face almost splitting into a grin. "It'll be just like old times."

Like most people who spent no time in Southeast Asia, I have an irrational, media-inflamed fear of Vietnam vets. They seem perfectly normal one minute, then up on the roof with a rifle the next. Or so goes the paranoia. Lord knows, I'd encountered enough weird vets during my peacetime stint in the U.S. Air Force a dozen years ago. Hellstrom, so inscrutably macho in his blue jumpsuit and his graying crew cut, worried me. What if he suddenly spotted Vietcong down on the prairie? What if he decided to end it all in the place he loved best, behind the stick of a chopper? What if—and this was the most likely scenario— I yarked all over his shiny helicopter? How would he react? I had a feeling I'd be left out here for buzzard bait.

I gulped and braced myself as Hellstrom whipped the chopper onto its side to swing east again, back toward the city. The ground zipped past directly below me, looking like an inviting place to throw up.

The mesa's crunkled western edge flitted past, a black snake among the tufts of yellow grass clinging to the topsoil that thinly veils the volcanic rock. The mesa is a broad crenelated fortress of frozen lava from the volcanoes that mark Albuquerque's western fringe. It rises steeply between two river basins: the Rio Grande valley, which is green and thickly populated, and the dry sparseness of the Rio Puerco.

Though it was only a couple of miles away, I couldn't see the city from this vantage. The volcano-studded crown of the mesa blocked the view. But I could see the Sandia Mountains beyond, a rugged wall of cliffs mottled with shadow under the high-noon sun. I longed to be back in Albuquerque, sitting under an air conditioner somewhere, maybe tipping back a beer, reading a paperback detective novel. But I'd promised Amber Field I'd find her husband, and zooming around the Rio Puerco with Reed Hellstrom seemed the only way to do it.

Amber had come seeking help the day before. Since my total caseload stood at an unhealthy zero, I'd been all ears.

Amber Field was in her mid-twenties, slender and leggy, with wide brown eyes and the air of someone accustomed to comfort. She had a fidget that seemed like a new acquisition, an edginess that was explained by the fact that her husband, a biologist named David Field, had been missing for three days. When she last saw him, David had been loading his Jeep with cameras and other gear for a day trip out to the Rio Puerco. He'd never returned.

She hadn't worried much at first. David sometimes camped overnight at his research sites. He was experienced and well equipped. But after a couple of nights without a word, Amber became convinced that something bad had happened to him.

Missing-person cases were nothing new to me. When you're trying to scratch out a living as a private investigator, lots of folks want you to turn up long-lost relatives or runaway kids or husbands who've skipped with their secretaries. I can't always find them, but I can milk a case for a good while, pulling down that daily retainer, plus expenses, before the grumbling client gives up.

When I look for somebody who's gone missing, I usually check the motels and the airport, credit card receipts, and my sources on the street. This one was different. David Field was supposed to be somewhere in this endless, empty land. An air search seemed the only way to go, and Amber was willing to pay for it.

Feeling no better than I do about flying, I'd been tempted to point Amber toward the nearest helicopter charter service and send her on her way. But I needed the money. Plus, Amber had been referred to me by someone whose opinion I valued above all others: my fiancée, Felicia Quattlebaum. Amber met Felicia at the *Albuquerque Gazette,* where she'd gone looking for help. As if she could turn up a missing hubby with a lost-and-found notice in the newspaper. Some editor referred Amber to my sweetie because Felicia had been writing a series of articles about the real estate boom along the Rio Puerco.

The experts predicted this vast nothingness just one mesa away from the big city would, over the next decade, sprout industry and neighborhoods, eventually becoming home to hundreds of thousands of people. Flying low over the sagebrush and the outcroppings of black basalt, I had trouble imagining anyone hiking out here, much less building a house. But you had only to look northeast to Rio Rancho to see it was possible.

Rio Rancho started as a suburban outpost of cheap houses and convenience stores. It now was officially the fastest-growing small town in America, fueled by computer-chip companies like Intel and Sumitomo that had located there from California in search of cheap workers who didn't join labor unions and cheap land that wasn't prone to earthquakes. Now, national magazines regularly carried stories about the boom on "Silicon Mesa."

Anytime there's money to be made in New Mexico, developers and corrupt politicians belly up to the trough, elbowing each other out of the way. Rio Puerco roughly translates to "Pig River," and that's a pretty apt description of the gluttony and greed surrounding the land boom. Felicia was having a field day tracking deeds and deals, naming names in stories for the front page.

Rabid as she was over her land investigation, Felicia couldn't be bothered with some missing biologist. I took it as a compliment that she'd thought to steer Amber Field my way. Praise from Felicia is such a rare commodity, I cling to every scrap.

Felicia's my toughest critic. She's so perceptive, so sharp, so *fierce* that most of the time I feel like a doofus just being around her. When I goof, I can always count on her to point it out. She'd taken it easier on me lately, maybe because I hadn't done anything really stupid recently. More likely, it was because the wedding was only ten days away. She probably didn't want to say or do anything that might make me bolt.

The thought of the wedding clenched my stomach, which didn't help my airsickness. Then Hellstrom yanked back on the stick, pulling the copter straight up and into a swooping curve.

"You see it?" his unexpected voice blared through the headphones into my ears.

"What? What?"

"The Jeep. Over there at three o'clock."

I hadn't even been looking at the ground. Good thing Hellstrom was more focused.

He slowed the chopper and wheeled it around, and I saw the dusty roof of a red Jeep Cherokee peeking over the edge of a shallow canyon that rippled downhill toward the Rio Puerco.

"I'll set down," Hellstrom grunted in my ears. "You can go check it out."

What could I say? No thanks, I don't like to walk around in the desert. I'm afraid of rattlesnakes. I'm afraid of what I might find in that Jeep. Don't you want to go with me? One glance over at Hellstrom, at that jaw jutting like a snowplow, told me the right answer: "Roger."

A cloud of blond dust engulfed the helicopter as the runners thumped onto the ground.

"Keep your head low," he said through the headphones.

I nodded, fumbled to unbuckle my seat belt. Then I was out the door, running under the dangerous whirring blades, holding my breath, and squinting against the dust.

Once clear of the dust cloud, I straightened up and walked toward the narrow canyon, what we call an arroyo out here. Arroyos are the work of summer thunderstorms—eroded channels that carry rushing water to riverbeds that might fill up only a couple of times a year. This time of year, late September, following a dry summer, rain seemed a distant memory to this land.

I stumbled over the clumps of dry grass, too busy watching for rattlers that might be sunning among the sparse vegetation to watch my own feet. I'm deathly afraid of snakes. Once, when I was fourteen, I stepped over a fallen tree limb in the woods near my Mississippi home and got nailed by a copperhead that lay in wait there. Mama got me to a doctor in time, but the snake's venom made me sick for a couple of weeks and turned my foot black. I recovered physically, but the snakebite damaged my psyche. Now, I can't even go into the reptile house at the zoo without getting a bad case of the shudders.

The copter's blades thudded to a stop behind me, and

silence descended on the desert. I glanced back, to find
Hellstrom still at the helm, watching me through the set-
tling dust. I remembered my gun, pulled it from the holster
clipped to my belt, gave him a manly nod. Then I took a
deep breath, scrambled down the arroyo, and approached
the Jeep.

No sign of anyone. I reached to open the door of the
vehicle, then thought of whooping car alarms and settled
for peering in the windows. Aside from a layer of gritty
dust, the interior was unremarkable. Behind the rear seats
sat an open cardboard box filled with a jumble of snacks,
notebooks, water jugs, and other gear.

I made my way around the Jeep, watching the ground
for footprints (and snakes), then eased downhill. The arroyo
curved south, then flattened out into a shallow, rock-dotted
pan where water had collected in the past. The ground was
riddled with burrows of some kind, dirt piled up around the
edges, and I carefully stepped around them, quaking against
the certainty that serpents thick as my arm occupied these
desert dwellings.

Thirty yards away, two gnarly junipers provided the only
semblance of shade for a mile in any direction. The ground
near one was charred black, and I strolled over, curious and
watchful. Nothing moved, not even a breeze. I squatted
near the edge of the onetime campfire, studied the ashes,
didn't like what I found there. Somebody had burned a
couple of cameras. The lenses were shattered, but their
scorched metal cases revealed them to be expensive Leicas.
A melted film canister lay near the edge of the fire, along
with a couple of curly black wires that once had been the
spines of spiral notebooks.

I got to my feet, looked around some more. Near the
base of the other tree, camouflaged so well I hadn't even
noticed, stood a small pup tent. I took it to be a blind of

the sort duck hunters use. It was only big enough for one person to squat inside, and I got a bad feeling about who might be in there.

I pointed my gun at the blind and edged closer. I glanced back once toward the helicopter, but the sun reflected off the dragonfly-eye windshield and I couldn't see Hellstrom. Still, the thought he was watching made me puff out my chest and stride right up to the tiny tent. I grabbed the door flap, yanked it up, and the whole tent lifted off the ground and tipped over. The floorless tent collapsed as I tried to catch it. The canvas was strung between two aluminum poles that nearly pierced me. I wrestled the thing around and tried to fold it, then finally threw it down a few feet away.

Lying on the ground was a corpse. He was facedown and the back of his head was a crusty mess of blackened blood. Between his shoulder blades, his tan cotton shirt was crunchy with the same substance. The desert was already working on the body, drying it out, turning it leathery.

I had the urge to run, but I fought it, knowing that Hellstrom, the Marlboro Man, watched. I had little doubt the lifeless stiff before me was David Field, but I had to go through the motions of making sure. I dramatically pulled from my shirt pocket the photograph of Field that his wife had supplied, which showed a deeply tanned man sitting in a rocker, smiling at the camera. He had a brow line like *The Thinker* and a chin like Cary Grant. A tan shirt like the one on the corpse was pulled tight across a thick chest. Rolled-up sleeves showed off hairy, sinewy forearms.

Bracing myself, I waved away the swarming flies and squatted down. I grabbed the corpse's heavy shoulder and lifted it slightly to get a look at his face. The bullets hadn't penetrated here, but scavengers had been at his eyes and nose and lips, leaving black holes where his features should've been. His mouth was pulled back in a maniacal grin. Red ants crawled around in his eye sockets. I felt my breakfast rising, and I tried to leap up, but it was too late. I vomited in David Field's face.

TWO

HELLSTROM'S REACTION when I showed him the body was a simple grunt that somehow said he'd seen worse. I detected a hint of amusement around his slit of a mouth over how the sight had affected me, which I didn't need. Then he marched back to the chopper to radio for help.

I looked around for some shade, the only place to wait in the desert. Not much to be had, with the sun almost directly overhead, and I wasn't staying by the junipers and Field's body. Over by the Jeep looked like my best bet, and I headed that way. My stomach hurt and I felt dizzy, and sweaty, and ashamed.

Suddenly, the air was filled with a dreaded buzzing. I froze, unsure which way to run, then snapped my head back and forth, looking for the rattler. The noise stopped, started again, and I was able to zero in on it. It wasn't a rattlesnake at all. A round head poked up from one of the burrows, its hooked beak open and its throat bobbing as it imitated a rattler. It had the fierce feathery eyebrows of a hawk, but its eyes were round and yellow, and I figured it for an owl of some kind. I walked toward it and it *cack-cacked* and stepped up out of the hole on long, skinny legs. It perched on the rim of its burrow and bobbed and bowed like a prizefighter, trying to look threatening. The bird was maybe ten inches tall and was dappled brown and tan and white, perfect for hiding out here. Plus, it could mimic a rattle-snake. Jeez, what a package.

Wildlife, I don't need. The desert's spooky enough without thinking about all the little creepy crawlers that make their living out here. I shouted, "Shoo!" and stomped my foot.

In a flash, the owl was in flight, zooming straight toward my head.

"Shit!"

I ducked into a squat as the bird wheeled away toward the junipers. I straightened up, hitched my jeans, hoping Hellstrom hadn't seen my encounter with nature. Then I trudged over to the Jeep to await the arrival of the law.

It took the sheriff's investigators an hour to reach the scene, even with Hellstrom guiding them by radio. He finally lifted off, flying over the deputies' vehicles to lead them directly to the site. I stayed near the Jeep, squatting in the sliver of shade, still shaken up over Field's corpse and what I had done to it.

The owl returned to its burrow to stand sentinel, and I noticed a couple of other owls farther away, doing the same. I felt like chucking rocks at them, but I didn't need to be dive-bombed again.

Finally, the deputies roared up in their four-wheel-drive patrol Broncos, ready to stake out a crime scene in the middle of freaking nowhere. They weren't going to like the way I'd messed up the evidence.

The first cop to approach had large ears that stuck out from his head, appearing to hold up his Stetson. He was lean and long-necked, and he wore mirrored sunglasses, which reflected my face when I shook his hand. First Hellstrom, now this guy. All day, it was as if I was talking to myself.

He identified himself as Lieutenant Erndow, lifted off the Stetson, and ran a handkerchief over a pointed bald head.

"What've we got here?" he asked.

"Dead guy name of David Field, over there by that tree. We were searching for him out here and we saw his car—"

"Let's go take a look."

"Uh, I'd just as soon keep my distance, if you don't mind."

Erndow pointed the mirrored sunglasses at me. I took it he was giving me the hard look, but who could tell? He shrugged and said, "Suit yourself."

He walked through the scrub toward the body, and I noticed he was wearing fancy brown cowboy boots that probably weren't regulation. His tan uniform was creased so sharply you could shave yourself with it, and he walked from the hips down, keeping his shoulders straight and thrown back. He made a slow circuit of the body, viewing it from all directions, then squatted down for a closer look.

The other three deputies who'd arrived in the two Broncos hung back, looking fat and round-shouldered compared with Erndow.

Erndow rose from his squat, came back my way, marching like John Philip Sousa.

"That your puke over there?"

I hung my head. "Yeah."

"Seems like you'd know better, this being a crime scene."

"It was, um, unexpected."

"I'll bet."

He paused, watching me.

"You got a permit for that gun you're carrying?"

I had forgotten about the revolver I'd slipped back into its holster.

"Yeah, at home. You wanna see my private investigator's license?"

Erndow shook his head.

"I've seen one before. That gun been fired?"

"Not in months."

"Mind if I see it?"

I handed it over and Erndow sniffed at the barrel, making me glad I'd cleaned it after the last time I'd taken target practice.

He handed the gun back to me and I holstered it without a word. Then Erndow turned to the deputies and said, "Okay, boys, go on over there and take whatever evidence you can find. Watch where you step."

The three deputies hustled over to Field's body. Erndow turned back to me, looked me over. I could feel the blush burning my cheeks. Dang, why'd I have to barf on the corpse? It put me on a bad footing with Erndow from the get-go.

Hellstrom had set the helicopter down a couple of hundred yards away, conscious of the dust he'd raise, and walked over. He joined us about then, and he and Erndow looked as if they were competing in a posture contest. I tried to stand up straighter, but my aching stomach muscles protested.

Recognizing Hellstrom as a fellow member of the He-Man Club, Erndow turned to him to ask his questions.

"How did you two find yourselves out here?"

Hellstrom gestured toward me with his Dick Tracy chin.

"This guy hired me this morning to hunt for somebody who was missing out here. Took us a little over an hour to find him."

"What did you do then?"

"I landed the bird and let him check it out. Once I saw what we had, I radioed you fellas."

Erndow paused, glanced my way.

"Guess it's back to you. How did you know he was out here?"

"I didn't for sure. I was hired by his wife yesterday to hunt him down. He'd been missing for three days. Last time he was seen, he'd been on his way out here. A helicopter seemed like a natural."

Erndow nodded me silent.

"Why didn't she go to the police?"

"She did, but she didn't think they were much help. They filed a missing person's report, put him on the computer, but nobody was going to comb all this empty out here unless she sprung for it."

"And that's where you came in." He wrote something in a pocket-sized notebook.

"Yeah. I told her it was a long shot, but she was willing to pay for the helicopter—"

"Speaking of which," Hellstrom interrupted, "the meter's still running. You want me to hang around here any longer?"

I looked to Erndow.

"You can go," he said to Hellstrom, "but the private eye stays."

Hellstrom gave us a brisk nod, turned on his heel, and strode off toward the helicopter. I found myself wishing, despite my earlier airsickness, that I was going with him.

"My truck's back at the airport," I said.

"We'll get you back there," Erndow said, smiling thinly. "Eventually."

THREE

ERNDOW AND I SPENT THE DAY together. Wish I could say we became friends, but every time he looked at me, it was as if his thoughts were a neon sign blinking in my head: Jeez, what a freaking screwup this guy is.

The day went like this: more questioning at the scene, with Erndow never cutting me any slack at all. A bumpy, miserable ride overland to the nearest roads, in Rio Rancho. Then a long, silent drive through the sprawling West Side and across the Rio Grande to downtown, where the sheriff's department shared a headquarters building with its big brother, the Albuquerque Police Department. More questioning there, and a couple of hours sitting around on a hard bench, waiting for the promised ride.

I might've had an easier time of it if I'd been dealing with the APD. At least I know people in the police department, might've been able to ask some favors, like a more comfortable seat. Dealing with Erndow and the rest in the sheriff's Criminal Investigations Division reminded me just how far afield I'd gone this time.

I had few answers for Erndow and his fellow inquisitors. What had David Field been doing out there? I don't know. What was with the burned cameras? I don't know. What could he have been photographing? Beats me. Why'd he park his Jeep in that arroyo, out of sight? I'm stumped.

Who would want him dead? That's a good one; you got me there.

The hardest part, though, was seeing Amber Field after she was summoned to headquarters to identify the body. All of Amber's perkiness had evaporated by the time she reached the cop shop. She looked like a wild woman, her long brown hair all over the place, her face screwed up tight, tears streaming down her cheeks. She could scarcely answer Erndow's questions for sobbing.

No surprise in that. Amber hadn't expected David to be dead. They never do. Plus, she seemed to be powerfully in love with the older man to whom she'd been married only two years. When she'd hired me, her description of him had been like something out of *The Bridges of Madison County.* David was a rugged outdoorsman. David was a free spirit. David had a Ph.D. from Cornell, you know, but he always wanted to work out west. David was in great physical shape, exercised every day. If anyone could survive out there, lost in the desert, it was David.

Yeah, well, David wasn't bulletproof. And Amber had a lot of trouble with that.

Only once did Erndow leave us alone. Amber sat beside me on the bench, dabbing at her face with shredded Kleenex, trying to breathe through the sobs and hiccups. I'm always awkward at times like these, but I patted her shoulder and made soothing noises. When she finally got herself under control, she turned her puffy face toward me.

"Mr. Mabry, I appreciate what you did to find David."

"Sure. I didn't—"

"Now I want you to find whoever killed him."

"What? Oh, well now, Mrs. Field, that's really a job for the police."

"They won't do anything," she said bitterly. "Just like they did nothing when I reported David missing. They've got hundreds of crimes to solve. You think they're going to put out any extra effort to find David's killer?''

"I'm sure they'll do everything—''

"They don't even have any clues. You said yourself it happened in a remote area. No witnesses. No evidence."

The thought of how I'd tainted whatever evidence might've been around David Field's face made my stomach knot. Maybe I owed her.

Tears leaked from her eyes. She took a deep, shuddery breath.

"Say you'll do it, Mr. Mabry. Say you'll help me."

What could I do? The cops wouldn't like me nosing around a murder case, but I couldn't turn down a freshly grieving widow. Plus, I needed the money to set up my new life as Felicia's husband.

"Sure, Mrs. Field. I'll do it. You can count on me."

Once Amber left the cop shop, a gum-chewing deputy drove me back over the mesa rim to retrieve my pickup from the Double Eagle Airport. I probably could've just left the truck there overnight, but it's only a couple of months old and I worry about someone stealing it or scratching the bright red paint. The truck is a beefy Dodge Ram with a tall chrome grille and broad-shouldered fenders. The Ram was a bequest from a grateful client, and I intended to take good care of it, despite the temptation to take for granted something I got for free.

As I drove across town to Felicia's apartment, I wondered how she would feel if somebody found me dead in the desert, wondered if it would wreck her the way David Field's death had crushed Amber. Hard to imagine Felicia getting that broken up over anything. And she sure didn't have the rosy view of me that Amber Field had of her husband. Knowing Felicia, her response probably would be something like "It was bound to happen one of these days."

FOUR

IT WAS PAST DINNERTIME when I got home. Felicia's apartment—I still thought of it that way, though I'd lived there two months—stood in a landscaped complex in the Northeast Heights, an area that rivals the desert in its sameness. Mile after mile of six-lane thoroughfares lined with fast-food joints and video shops and "I can't believe they stay in business" storefronts offering everything from tropical fish to chain saws.

I'd vowed never to reside up here, in the Land of the Almighty Auto, the Sunbelt version of Levittown. I'd lived for years in the Desert Breeze Motor Inn on East Central Avenue, old Route 66, and if I could claim roots anywhere, it was there, in the red-light district known as the Cruise. Felicia and I had nearly gone our separate ways over my determination to stay among the grifters and the drifters and the street crazies of the Cruise, but situations change, and a person has to adapt.

My situation changed in a big way, overnight. Not long after Felicia had decided to lay off about where I lived and accept that I needed certain surroundings, the owner of the Desert Breeze, Bharat "Bongo" Patel, announced he was selling the old motel and moving to California. The new owners were big-bellied Texans who favored boots and ten-gallon hats with their double-knit suits. Not my kind of people. They planned to paint the place a color other than

Bongo's favored hot pink, gussy it up, and play to the growing trade of nostalgia nuts who wanted a true Route 66 experience. If that experience included getting mugged, they'd be in the right place.

The new owners definitely didn't want permanent residents. I'd lived at the Desert Breeze for nearly a decade, and Bongo had never raised my rent because he depended on having someone like me, experienced and well armed, to back him up whenever some hophead or hooker got out of line. The new owners sent me a letter saying the rent would double on the first of August and triple by the end of the year. They wanted me out, and there wasn't a damned thing I could do about it.

I might've moved to another motel along the Cruise, but most of them were in even worse shape than the Desert Breeze. Hookers whooping through thin walls, leaky roofs, and used syringes littering the parking lot eventually become oppressive, even for a forgiving sort like me.

Felicia had offered to take me in, as if I was stray cat or something, and it only made sense. I spent a lot of nights with her anyway. Why pay two rents?

Her frilly mauve apartment swallowed up my meager possessions so completely that I still wasn't sure where everything had gone. It had taken me about a week to admit that functioning air conditioning, modern appliances, and carpeting were all desirable accoutrements.

It took about another week, after a particularly energetic bout of lovemaking in Felicia's queen-sized bed, for me to pop the question. I'd been thinking about marriage for some time, off and on, mostly with the mixture of dread and anxiety that would accompany a different kind of decision, like whether to take up hang gliding or bungee jumping. But in that weakened moment, my breath still coming hard from sex in four different positions, the question just slipped out of my mouth like air out of a balloon.

As soon as I said it, I wished to retrieve the words, to take it all back. But Felicia doesn't miss much, and she certainly wouldn't let something as momentous as that go by unnoticed. That she'd immediately responded yes told me she'd been thinking about it, too, though I'm sure she would've denied it if cornered.

Of course, there was no sleeping after that. We had to put on our bathrobes and look at a calendar and set a date and call her parents in Indiana and tell them the good news, though it was past midnight there. Plans had to be made, from venue to menu, from gowns to cakes to bridal registries. Felicia had seemed ready to go all night, planning every detail. Only when my head slumped back and I started to snore did she call it a night.

The planning frenzy hadn't ended that night. Felicia is a creature of raging enthusiasms. Once she gets hold of something—whether it be a land scam or a wedding plan— she busies it to death.

I accepted her every demand in exchange for her agreeing to one from me: We had to move. I couldn't stand the Northeast Heights long-term and wanted to be closer to my pals on the Cruise. Plus, the apartment was her place; everything about it was hers, from the furniture to the panty hose drying on the shower curtain rod. I needed neutral territory to feel that we were starting up a new life together, as equals.

We'd begun the search for a rental house, but in a boomtown like Albuquerque, where home prices rise faster than incomes, lots of people want to rent, and homes were in short supply.

I read an article that said moving and getting married are two of the highest stress producers a person can experience.

To get any more stressed-out, I'd need a death in the family and to get fired from a job. Fortunately, I'm self-employed. And if anybody in my family stood at risk of sudden death, it was probably me.

I swung the big Dodge into the parking lot of Felicia's apartment compound and found an open slot around the corner from her stairwell. The apartments had reserved slots covered by carportlike roofs, but my Ram wouldn't fit under them. Another strike against Mountain Shadows Apartments.

Though the sun had slipped below the horizon, the asphalt still cooked from the heat of the day, spongy under my sneakers. I tucked at my shirttail and ran my hands through my thinning brown hair, trying to get presentable before seeing my sweetie. Probably wasn't much help. I'd sweated through my clothes during the day, and I could feel desert grit on my forehead. I was tired and hungry and more than a little grumpy. I certainly wasn't ready for what I found when I swung open the door to Felicia's apartment.

Every surface in the living room was covered with two-foot-long strips of cloth—brocades, ginghams, plaids, and paisleys; chenilles, flannels, and corduroys; rayon, nylon, Dacron. It looked an explosion at Fabric World.

"What the—"

"Hi, honey!" Felicia came bounding from the bedroom, more fabric strips draped over both arms.

"What's all this?"

"Samples. We've got some decisions to make."

Felicia's eyes looked wide and fevered behind the square plastic glasses that had slipped down her nose. Her hair—normally a dark waterfall of sheen bobbed just clear of her shoulders—was standing out from her head from static electricity. She wore familiar clothes: jeans, sneakers, and a plain white bowling shirt with *Larry* embroidered on the chest. But the dangling fabric samples gave her giant harlequin sleeves of clashing colors and competing patterns. A Virginia Slim dangled from the side of her mouth, bouncing as she talked, a dangerously long finger of ash on the end. I'd already seen a corpse today. I didn't need to see Felicia burst into flames.

"I was talking with Denise, and she said we just haven't covered enough territory when it comes to curtains and comforters and towels."

Denise was the woman in charge of the bridal registry at Dillard's department store. She and Felicia apparently had become fast friends in the past couple of weeks. All I heard was "Denise this" and "Denise that." If Denise worked on commission, she must be making a fortune.

The whole bridal registry deal eluded me. It was like shopping without buying anything. No, it was weirder than that. It was shopping for things that other people would buy for you. We'd already covered dish designs and silverware patterns and electronic gizmos for the kitchen. I'd gone along as best I could, trying to act interested each time Felicia brought home a catalog or a trunkload of samples from which we'd choose. These were lifetime decisions, Felicia always reminded me, and I could hear the echo of the mysterious Denise. These were the items we'd use in our household forever.

The fact that we didn't have a household, that we couldn't find a house to hold, was beside the point. Wherever we ended up living, we'd need these things, Felicia argued. And if friends or relatives were willing to pony up their hard-earned cash to buy us, say, a toaster, then we, by God, ought to tell them which one we liked best.

The great unspoken in all this, I feared, was that I, Bubba Mabry, didn't make enough money to furnish my own home. Felicia made a good living at the *Gazette*, but not enough to keep both of us in food and rent and new toasters besides. My income was sporadic at best. Depending on my earnings was as iffy as depending on the kindness of strangers. Felicia seemed to believe we had a chance here to make a killing on household goods, and it was an opportunity we weren't going to squander.

Felicia talked on, holding up one arm, then the other, gesturing towards particular samples with her cigarette.

"So I was thinking this maroon for the bath, to kind of give some contrast, see? Then, in the kitchen, going with some other shade of red. Denise says reds are very popular now. They really brighten a room. Now, in the bedroom—"

I tuned her out. I hadn't eaten anything since breakfast, and I'd managed to lose that meal all over David Field. My legs ached with fatigue. My head hurt from a full day of Erndow's interrogation. What I needed was quiet and food and booze and rest and sympathy, not some nightmare from the Home Shopping Network.

"You're not listening, are you?"

"What? No, I'm sorry. Guess I'm not."

Felicia rolled her eyes. Then her gaze hardened and she set her jaw. I knew that look. It usually made me cringe, but I was too tired.

"Bubba, I know you don't care about this stuff, but I need your help. If you're going to be an equal partner—"

"I found a dead body today."

"Then you've got to—what?"

"Corpse. Found one. In the desert. Ugly."

That gave her pause.

"The biologist?"

"Yup. Dead. Ants parading around in his eye sockets."

Felicia made a face. In the course of her career, she'd probably seen more manglings, murders, and all-around mayhem than I'd ever care to witness, but that was enough to gross out even her. And she knew how such sights bothered me.

"Poor baby. You been with the cops all day?"

I nodded, tried to look pitiful.

"You must be exhausted."

More nods. "Hungry, too."

Felicia dropped her arms, let all the fabric slip to the floor. The cigarette ash dropped on it, but she didn't seem to notice as she snatched the butt from her mouth and stubbed it out in an overflowing ashtray.

"Let's get you fixed up. You just sit down. I'll make you a sandwich and you can tell me all about it."

I looked helplessly around at all the furniture, trying to spot a clear place where sitting wouldn't wrinkle some important shopping decision.

"Just throw that shit on the floor," Felicia said over her shoulder as she hustled off to the apartment's small kitchen. I wasn't about to throw anything anywhere. I didn't want to touch anything, for fear it might be interpreted as an expression of interest in a particular fabric. I settled onto one of the two stools that faced the waist-high counter separating the kitchen from the living room. I rested my elbows on the bar and rested my forehead on my hands.

"You wanna beer?" she asked as she opened the fridge and peered inside. I was surprised to see there weren't fabric samples in there, too.

"Bourbon."

"Coming right up."

A glass of ice cubes and a bottle of Jim Beam appeared in front of me and I poured a stiff one.

"So, the biologist—what's his name?"

"David Field."

"Right. Somebody offed him?"

Felicia has such a sweet way about her.

"Yeah, coupla slugs in the head, one in the back."

She straightened up from the fridge, bread, Oscar Mayer ham, and a jar of mayo in her hands.

"Been dead long?"

"Yeah, I think so. Listen, can we not talk about it right now? My appetite, you know."

"Sure, hon. You just sit there and rest a minute while I whip up some chow."

I nodded, sighed.

"And then, when you feel better, you can tell me what you think of a comforter patterned in shades of teal."

FIVE

I GOT AN EARLY START the next morning. The working people of New Mexico consider every Friday to be something of a holiday, and I figured it was no different at the University of New Mexico. Maybe I could catch some people in their offices before they all took off for a jump start on the weekend.

It took a while to locate the Biology Department. First, I had to find a place to park the Ram, a test harder than any exam in, say, quantum physics. Parking lots were coded according to permits, and every time I found a likely spot, it was only to discover I didn't have the proper B sticker or G stamp. I finally nailed a space at a parking meter, which I stuffed with every quarter in my possession.

The university resembles a landscaped Indian pueblo, with multistory buildings uniformly plastered in shades of mud. The older, round-shouldered buildings even have vigas jutting out from the rooflines. Newer buildings have the look of boondoggles some smart-ass architect pulled on whoever paid to throw them up: modern, sharp-shinned buildings with balconies in odd places and strips of glass meant to approximate windows. All the buildings were labeled with turquoise-colored signs, but I didn't see anything that said BIOLOGY or THE OFFICE OF DAVID FIELD.

I wandered up a broad walkway tiled in circular patterns, admiring the late-blooming flowers and emerald lawns that bordered the buildings. There were other distractions, as well. The place teemed with students, including migrating flocks of coeds with smooth brown skin, wearing cutoffs and halter tops. I caught myself staring, and I thought of Felicia. She wouldn't like that. The males were almost as gazeworthy, with their dreadlocks and tattoos, bare chests and sandals. Hormones hung thick in the air. It was as if I'd stumbled onto some primitive tribe that ate their elders.

I felt conspicuous. I was the only one in sight without a backpack filled with books, the only one with lines on my face, the only one who looked as if he didn't spend every waking moment at a gym. The shirtless males were especially intimidating, with their bulging arms and washboard stomachs. I have a washtub stomach.

Sometimes I think I'm the only man in North America who doesn't lift weights. I'll do a few push-ups occasionally, just to keep my blood moving, but weights? Get outta here. I try not to do any heavy lifting when someone's paying me, much less for *fun*. In fact, I'm prejudiced against guys with lots of muscles. I figure they spend more time working on their bodies than on their brains and therefore are more stupid and more superficial than I am. At the same time, I fear them. I may be superior to them, but they could still kick my butt. Bravado results from such mixed feelings. Faced with a big, stupid guy, it's hard for me not to trot out my smarts and show them off. Big, stupid guys aren't impressed by that. They see it as kicking verbal sand in their faces.

I picked one of the smaller natives to approach on the campus. He was a boy about half my age, and he wore his hair shaved on the sides and long on top, dropping down to a thick black ponytail in the back. It looked like an animal squatting on his head. He had a few wispy whiskers, a gold chain around his neck, and the briefest of cutoff jeans decorated with patches and strategic rips. When I said, "Excuse me," he gave me a brush-off look, as if I was trying to sell him something or bum a dime.

"Excuse me?" I said again, stepping sideways to prevent his escape. "Can you direct me to the Biology Department?"

His eyes narrowed.

"I don't know, man. I'm new here. Try over there."

He jerked his head backward and to the right, then huffed away.

I walked in the direction he'd indicated, past clumps of chatting students who loitered on the lush lawns. I saw a building labeled GEOLOGY, but not BIOLOGY. Then I spotted it, tucked back in the corner of a small sycamore-shaded plaza. CASTETTER HALL, the sign read, BIOLOGY.

I was looking forward to some air conditioning by the time I'd hotfooted it across the plaza to the entrance. No wonder all the students go around with no clothes. My jeans stuck to my legs and the back of my shirt clung to my shoulder blades. But I found no cooling artificial breeze when I stepped through the door of the building. Instead, I was hit by a wall of humidity that reminded me of the weather back home in Mississippi.

"Jeez, what's with this place?" I muttered.

Behind a sweating glass wall, a jumble of plants and trees filled a room two stories high—a greenhouse. I pressed against the glass, peering inside at the potted palms and ferns and whatnot. The room was dominated by a towering evergreen of some sort I'd never seen, perfectly symmetrical, reaching in all directions with branches that looked soft.

I turned away quickly when someone came through the door behind me. It was a chunky girl—they had fat people on this campus?—who was red-faced and puffing from exertion. She blew past me, probably late for class, and disappeared down a hallway. I followed, pushing through another door and finally finding some relief from the heat. Air-conditioned corridors ran in two directions, lined with closed doors and walls of swirly frosted glass you could almost see through. A sign above one door said, ADMINISTRATION, and that sounded like a destination to me.

The svelte woman at the front desk had been crying. Her eyes were red and she was looking in a pocket mirror, trying her best to redo her mascara. She had a pile of thick black hair and chocolate eyes and enough makeup for two or three women, including lipstick that matched her dress, a shade I'd call Radioactive Red. The office reeked of perfume and hair spray. A lot of men would look at her and get aroused. The first thought that popped into my head was: High-maintenance.

The nameplate on her desk read MONICA GALLEGOS.

"Miss Gallegos?" I ventured as I approached.

"Yes?" She didn't take her eyes off the mirror. Whatever I might need could wait.

"My name's Bubba Mabry. I'm a private investigator, looking into the death of David Field."

That got her attention. Her head whipped toward me, her lower lip began to tremble, and tears sprang to her eyes. A gut-wrenching sob exploded from deep inside her, and she snatched up Kleenex to try to save her mascara.

"I take it you knew Mr. Field."

She nodded quickly, afraid to open her mouth and let out the bawling.

"I'd like to talk to people here who knew him and knew about his work—his boss, his colleagues, maybe you."

She shook her head vigorously, and I understood that she couldn't talk about him right now. She swiveled in her chair and pointed behind her, where offices opened off a short hallway. I nodded, thanked her, and walked in that direction. Sobs burst out behind me, but I didn't turn around. I didn't want to make it worse.

The door at the end of the hall bore a sign that said ANNA LIPSCOMB, DEPARTMENT CHAIR, and that seemed a good place to start. I knocked and entered when a woman called out from inside.

Anna Lipscomb was a plain-looking woman who was trying for ugly. She was tall and reedy, and she had her mousy hair trapped in a tight bun. She wore thick-lensed horn-rimmed glasses in a style that might've been cool in 1960. She stood, showing off a dog-tick gray blouse and matching trousers.

"May I help you?"

I went through my spiel again. Her lips disappeared when I said Field's name, but she caught herself and stopped frowning.

"And who employed you to conduct this investigation?"

Normally, I wouldn't reveal such information, but what could it hurt in this case?

"Mrs. Field."

"Ah, Amber. I see. Won't you sit down?"

A ratty orange armchair leaned in the corner, and I dragged it over and gingerly lowered myself into it.

"This won't take long, I presume," she said. "Where shall we begin?"

Since the clock was ticking, I started in with the big questions first.

"Why would anybody want to kill David Field?"

"I assure you, I have no idea. David was, in many ways, a model professor. The students enjoyed his classes and he was a dedicated researcher."

"Any problems in his personal life?"

"I wouldn't know. We had a strictly professional relationship."

I couldn't imagine her having any other kind.

"Any idea what he might've been doing out in the boonies?"

"From what the sheriff's deputy told me, it sounds like research of some sort, but he had told me nothing about it."

"What makes you think it was research?"

She made the prune face again, impatient.

"His body was found in a blind. His cameras were there, notebooks. Or so the deputy said."

I nodded.

"Those are tools David would have used to study some organism in the wild."

"But you don't know what it might've been?"

"No, I don't. You have to understand, Mr....Mabry, was it? You have to understand, Mr. Mabry, that David Field was something of a loner when it came to research. He didn't collaborate, he didn't share until he was ready."

"Keeping all the glory to himself?"

She almost smiled.

"The glory to be had in biological research is hardly fame and fortune. Mostly, we write papers read only by other biologists. This department gets a lot of money from the federal government for research—I'm proud to say we're one of the top departments in the nation—but the money all goes to equipment and lab techs and fieldwork, not to line anybody's pockets."

I tried to look properly chastised.

"No, David Field kept to himself because that was just his way. David was something of a Renaissance man of biology. His specialty was the desert Southwest, but he could speak intelligently about marine life or African ecology or whatever else you might want to discuss.''

"Sounds like he'll be hard to replace."

She looked smug for an instant.

"We'll miss him immeasurably."

I was running out of questions, but I still didn't have much of a picture of David Field as a person, what he was like before somebody snuffed him in the desert.

"You know Amber Field?"

Anna Lipscomb stiffened ever so slightly.

"Yes, of course. Amber was a student in this department."

"Is that so? Is that how she and David met?"

"Yes. Amber was a graduate student when she did some fieldwork for David."

"Did their relationship cause a scandal?"

"Hardly," she said coldly. "These things happen at universities. It's something of a closed society. People tend to begin relationships with those they know well."

I guessed Anna Lipscomb had managed to avoid such entanglements. Her closest relationship probably was with the computer that hummed on her desk.

"How was Amber as a student?"

"Very bright. A good future, I think. But she decided she'd rather be married to David than pursue her education further."

A little disdain dripped in there.

"I'd like to look through David Field's office, see if there's anything that might indicate what he was doing out there in the middle of nowhere."

"I'm afraid that wouldn't be possible."

"Why not?"

"It would be an invasion of David's privacy. He kept his office locked for a reason."

"Yeah, well, he's not around to object, is he?"

Anna Lipscomb rose to her full height without leaving her chair and looked down her nose at me.

"I said no."

"What happens to the stuff in his office now that he's dead?"

"I suppose it will go to Amber, just like any other inheritance he might've left. But I'm sure she's in no condition now—"

"I'll get her permission to search the place. I'll have her call you."

Her lips did that in-and-out number, but she couldn't think of another argument. "Very well."

"In the meantime, do you mind if I talk to some of the other teachers, see if they know anything?"

"Not at all. But do keep it brief. People are trying to work here."

"Yes, ma'am."

I left her my card and let myself out, wondering whether Anna Lipscomb would call ahead, warn everybody else away from me. I glanced back over my shoulder as the door swung closed. She was typing away furiously at her computer. No sign of her lips.

Monica Gallegos had vanished from her desk, so there would be no questioning her. I wandered off down the hall, looking for open office doors. I found one, knocked.

A man at the desk inside looked up from some papers, peering at me over his half glasses with startlingly blue eyes. His bristly gray hair was receding from a lined forehead and he sported a bushy white beard.

"Yes?"

I told him who I was, what I wanted. He invited me inside. He didn't so much stand as unfold from the chair, rising up, up, up, to a height of maybe six and a half feet.

He was dressed like a cowboy, in a plaid short-sleeve shirt and jeans with a large turquoise belt buckle. He was slim, but he had thick forearms and he nearly pulverized my hand when he shook it.

"Richard Slagg's my name, but everybody calls me Doc."

Doc Slagg. Sounded like a character out of Sgt. Rock comics. But I wasn't about to say that to this weathered giant.

He sat, pulled off the half glasses.

"So you're investigating David Field's tragic death? Sounds like a job for the police."

"They're doing it, too, but Field's wife asked me to make sure it doesn't get lost in the shuffle down at the sheriff's department."

He nodded, thinking.

"I suppose it was inevitable."

"What's that? Field getting murdered?"

"I told a deputy the same thing this morning. You dip your wick into enough lanterns, eventually you get burned."

"I'm not following you."

A light danced in his blue eyes.

"David Field was a notorious cocksman. Sorry if that shocks you, but I'm not one to mince words."

"Nothing shocks me anymore." But it had, and it probably showed on my face. Amber Field had described her husband as such romance-novel perfection, it hadn't occurred to me that maybe he'd been running around on her.

I found my voice, asked Slagg if Field had been putting it to anyone in particular.

Slagg shrugged.

"Don't know. But there's been a steady stream of them over the years. Hell, he even met his wife that way. I thought when he married Amber, he might settle down, but I've seen him with a couple of coeds in the past two years, and they looked like more than just workmates.''

"Can you give me names?"

The eyes twinkled again.

"No, I don't think so. You're the detective. You track 'em down.''

I didn't like that, but what could I do? Pull out my gun and force him to talk? I didn't even have the Smith & Wesson with me.

"Okay, then, what can you tell me about Field as a researcher? Was he as good as they say?''

Doc Slagg pursed his lips.

"Well, of course, I don't know what 'they' have been saying, do I? But Field was damned good. He could've been department chairman one of these days, once Old Tightass moves on, or he could've become nationally known for some of his desert research."

"Like what?"

"Global warming. Environmental change. The desert's a good barometer of such things because it's so fragile. If Field had buckled down, there's no telling what he would've found out there."

"But he didn't buckle down?"

"Oh, he worked hard, don't get me wrong. But I think he spent nearly as much time dipping his wick. Distraction is the enemy of good science."

"And you think those distractions got him killed."

Doc Slagg leaned back in his chair, steepled his fingers in front of him.

"That's my best guess. What else could it be? You don't follow somebody all the way out to the Rio Puerco and shoot him full of holes because he cut you off in traffic.

Murder, I think, takes rage. David Field knew how to bring that out in a woman.''

My head hummed. I needed time to adjust to this new vision of the victim.

''Any idea what he was doing out there?''

''None. Could've been most anything. Field and I weren't close. And he kept his projects to himself. Normally, you get two biologists in a room together and pretty soon they're plotting a joint research project. But not Field. He'd never mentioned anything about that area to me. We've got a big desert research station about sixty miles south of here. He could've done his work there. But no, he was out west of town, all alone, getting himself killed.''

''Doesn't sound like you're mourning him much.''

''Like I said, we weren't close. I was surprised at first, but once I thought about Field's dalliances, it all began to make sense.''

''Are there other faculty members who knew him better?''

''Maybe. You might try Emil Pugh, downstairs in the museum. He worked with David. Works with all of us, preparing specimens we bring in from the field. Strange little man, but he might know something.''

I thanked Slagg for his time, suffered another brutal handshake, then made my way to the stairs.

At the bottom of the stairs, I found blank gray doors at the end of a hall. There was a little sign saying MUSEUM OF SOUTHWEST BIOLOGY. The doors were locked, so I pounded on them until someone came.

The door was opened by a squat, stoop-shouldered man with shiny black hair parted in the middle. Peter Lorre eyes. But I couldn't keep my attention on him for the spectacle beyond.

Dead animals were everywhere. Stuffed trophy heads of

antelope and deer and elk peered out from the walls. Snarling skeletons crouched on top of tables and cabinets. Hawks were frozen in midswoop, talons extended. Elephant tusks crossed against one wall.

"Jeez."

"What it is that you want?"

I dragged my gaze back to the greasy little man before me. He still held the edge of the door with a stubby hand, and he looked ready to slam it in my face.

"I, uh, I—"

"The museum is closed to the public," he said sharply. "I'm very busy."

He tried to shut the door, but I got a foot in the way.

"Hold on a second. I'm a private investigator, asking questions about David Field."

That brought him up short—shorter.

"Why didn't you say so? Come in."

I wasn't sure I wanted to enter, not with all those lifeless eyes staring down from the walls, but Pugh seemed accustomed to it. He turned and waddled away. I followed.

Pugh wore a lab coat that fell almost to his knees. It had once been white, but it hadn't seen a washer in a long time.

I gawked my way down a corridor between wooden lockers divided into flat drawers, then turned a corner, to find Pugh already at work at a wide steel sink, stripping the skin off a blunt-tailed orange-speckled Gila monster.

"Is that what I think it is?"

Pugh looked up at me, then back down at the lizard. He made a wheezing sound that I took to be a laugh.

"This is old George. He lived in a display case upstairs for many years. I think he died a couple of days ago, but Gila monsters are so sluggish, who can tell?"

"You gonna stuff him?"

"I could, couldn't I?" The wheeze sounded again. "I

could put him back in his cage and nobody would ever know he was dead.''

"You do all this taxidermy?'' I gestured toward the dozens of animals that stared down at us.

"Not all of it. Some. It's my specialty. But we don't do much mounting anymore. Not politically correct, you know. We just preserve the parts and put them in drawers with numbers on them for research.''

That would explain the rows of lockers. It gave me the willies knowing the cabinets contained thousands of dead critters. I took a deep breath, pulled my little notebook from my hip pocket, and tried to look like a researcher myself.

"What can you tell me about David Field?''

"David, such a joker. I'm gonna miss him. He used to kid me, say he wanted me to stuff him after he died. Stand him in a corner here just to startle the undergrads.''

Pugh let loose another wheezing laugh. If he kept doing that, I was going to punch him.

"I don't suppose the police will turn his body over to me, though, do you?''

I gaped at him until he let his eyes go round and snickered some more. Gotcha.

"Look, do you know why Field might've been murdered?''

"No, not really. Could've been vandals or thieves. If you go out in the desert all by yourself, the biggest danger is other people. Roaming psychos, eh?''

"Maybe a psycho, not thieves. They burned his expensive cameras, didn't touch his Jeep.''

Pugh shrugged his round shoulders.

"I wouldn't know about that. I rarely go out in the desert myself. I prefer my wildlife dead and mounted and indoors. Beauty can be preserved without the danger, the unpredictability.''

Sheesh.

"I was talking to Doc Slagg upstairs. He said Field had a lot of illicit romances."

Pugh frowned, rubbed at his pale cheeks. He needed a shave.

"That Slagg. He's just jealous. He always thought David was too flashy, too fun, to be a good scientist. I say, if you can't have some fun, go do something else."

If Pugh's idea of fun was hanging out in a museum full of death, it might be time for him to consider a career change, too. The place, and its wheezing little denizen, gave me the creeps. I closed my notebook, handed Pugh my card.

"Thanks for your time. If you think of anything, call me."

"Sure thing. Now I must get back to work. Old George is waiting. Heh-heh."

I hustled out of there, up the stairs, back outside into the hot sunshine and the herds of students. I felt as if I'd escaped something.

Felicia regularly opines that I need to handle more cases like these, ones with a higher-class clientele, not people as strange or dangerous as the miscreants and misfits with whom I normally associate. These academic types might not be dangerous, but they had the market cornered on weird. Give me a street thug any day. I might get killed, but at least I don't have to worry about my body being stuffed and exhibited for eternity.

SIX

WHAT COULD BE MORE nerve-racking than being the only man in a roomful of women? It's like being the only monkey at the zoo, with all the people standing around, studying your habits. Or maybe turn that around: the only human in a cage full of lionesses.

Normally, I'd give such a situation the quickest of skips. But I needed Amber Field's permission to search her late husband's office. And it occurred to me I might learn something from the women who crowded around her, offering sympathy, food, drink.

I arrived at Amber's home in Spruce Park, just west of the university, first thing Saturday morning. The night before had been uneventful. I'd gone home after my encounters with the biologists at UNM, to find that fabric samples still littered the apartment. Felicia got home late from work, frazzled and too tried to make me decide about place mat patterns and napkin rings for Our Future Together. Felicia had Saturday off, and she seemed ready to spend the day with her new best friend, Denise, at the Bridal Registry, so I decided I might as well keep after the Field case.

Spruce Park dates to the 1920s and 1930s, when the faculty at the young university grew and created neighborhoods nearby. Some of the neighborhoods had become student ghettos over the years, surreal mixtures of shabby houses painted in psychedelic graffiti, dim coffee bars,

Deadhead buses, and monstrous apartment complexes squeezed onto narrow lots. But not Spruce Park. With its elm-arched streets and its mix of tidy houses, Spruce Park maintained the elegance of a well-bred old lady.

The Fields' home could've been lifted up from a street in Smallville and plunked down in Albuquerque. A brick cottage with a pitched roof, it would've looked out of place anywhere in New Mexico except here in Spruce Park.

I should've been tipped off to what was happening inside from the number of jewel-colored cars parked along the curb. But I blundered my way up to the door and rang the bell.

The front porch had been enclosed to make a sunroom and the interior door stood open, so I knew someone was inside. But it took a minute before a woman appeared and glided toward me. It wasn't Amber Field. In fact, I'd never seen this woman before. I would've remembered.

She had one of those bodies that seem determined to burst whatever clothes encased her. A flowered blue dress that should've seemed modest stretched itself over ample hips and breathtaking breasts, with their promise of what some poet once called "pneumatic bliss." She had a mane of red hair, parted on the side, sweeping over and almost covering one of her big green eyes. A sprinkling of freckles over a pert nose. An impish smile.

She gave me a spritely "Hi!"

I replied like this: "Gaaa—"

Her smile widened. She was accustomed to feeble men like me. My eyes swept over her like searchlights. I could feel my mouth hanging open.

"What's your name, little boy?" There was a trace of a southern accent.

"Bu-Bu-Bu-Bubba. Bubba Mabry."

"Hi there, Bubba. I'm Etta Dangler. Do you want to come in?"

Not trusting my mouth, I nodded quickly.

She swung open the screen door and held it for me, so that I had to pass within inches of her. I inhaled her scent—jasmine and nightshade—and nearly lifted off the ground. I felt light-headed, and I realized that no blood was getting to my brain. It was all busy elsewhere.

Etta let her eyes roam me, pausing briefly at the old bulging blood bank, and then met my gaze with a smile like a secret.

"Are you a friend of Amber's?"

"Amber? Oh, yeah, Amber. Amber Field. I'm here to see Amber."

"You a friend of hers?" she repeated, not breaking the eye lock with me.

"I'm Bubba Mabry. Oh, I said that already, didn't I? I'm a, uh, private investigator. Amber hired me to investigate the, uh, death."

"Well, then, I guess you better go in there and find her."

I blinked, looked around, saw we were still on the sunporch. I heard feminine voices emanating from the house's dim interior.

"Who's in there?"

"Amber's friends. We've been bringing her food and stuff all morning. You hungry?" She stretched out the last word just enough to load it with meaning.

"Always."

"Good. Enough casseroles and salads in there to feed an army. No sense in it going to waste. Bring your manly appetite right on in."

I followed her inside, bobbing in her wake like a buoy, staring at her ass, which was like a ripe plum.

Just inside the door, I froze. A dozen women filled the

room, standing, sitting, gathered around Amber by a table loaded down with Tupperware and aluminum foil-covered dishes. Conversation died as they all stared at the monkey in their midst.

"Everyone, this here's Bubba Mabry, Amber's private eye," Etta Dangler announced. "He came to see Amber, but I told him he ought to eat something while he's here."

I nodded and waved and grinned and generally acted like a galoot.

A couple of the other women flashed smiles at me, interested looks. They were uniformly young and attractive and well dressed, though none of them held a candle to Etta's scarlet tresses and sumptuous figure.

Amber looked like hell. She wore a white flannel bathrobe trimmed in lace around the collar and cuffs. She'd dragged a brush through her long brunette hair at some point, but she'd tangled it up again running her fingers through it. Her eyes were red and puffy and her face was splotchy and free of makeup. She held a wineglass in one hand and a wadded tissue in the other.

I tried to approach her, but her friends closed ranks. I felt Etta gently grasp my elbow.

"No business yet," she said just above a whisper. "Have something to eat."

It seemed awfully early in the morning for three-bean salad and tuna casserole. Normally, I can barely choke down anything more than coffee before about noon. But I dutifully loaded a paper plate and drifted toward the kitchen beyond. Etta Dangler followed, which helped my appetites but not my interest in food.

Some women are natural-born flirts, particularly southern women. They stand too close. They touch your arm a lot. They watch you out of the corners of their eyes, toss their hair, show their teeth. It's all primal, animalistic behavior,

I'm sure, worthy of a study by those bent biologists I'd interviewed the day before. It drives me crazy. Felicia's not like that. You always know where you stand with Felicia. She doesn't try to lure you unless she means it. She's straightforward about her desires and her needs. It's more honest, I think, more fair. But some women don't care about fairness. Something inside them wants men to jump up and run around and lose their minds. They want men to fall all over themselves, salivating over the possibilities; then they saunter away, leaving the men deflated and doubting themselves.

I've tried to overcome such stupidity over the years, part of a personal campaign to eliminate my genetic gullibility from my life. But here I was, gone gaga over Etta Dangler and her many charms. I told myself to pull together, to keep my wits sharp and my thoughts above the waist. She touched my hand and something melted inside me.

"Where you from, sugar?"

"Here. I live here."

"No, I mean originally. I hear a little South in your speech."

"Oh, right. Yeah. I'm from Mississippi originally. But I've been out here fifteen years."

"Isn't that something? I'm from Alabama myself, but I only came west a couple of years ago."

Conversation. Good. Keep dancing. Stick and move. Keep your mind on your work and your eyes off Etta Dangler's bountiful body.

"What brought you out here?"

"A man."

"Oh."

"He's gone now. It didn't work out."

"Too bad."

"I don't know. There are other men."

Yes, there are, I thought, and I'll bet you run through them like a freaking black widow spider.

"How do you know Amber?"

"Friend of a friend. We met at some faculty party and we've grown close. It's so sad about David."

I nodded, glanced beyond Etta toward the dining room. Amber was sitting now, and two of her friends hovered behind her, patting her shoulders.

I dropped my voice to a whisper. "Somebody told me David hadn't always been faithful."

A smile teased the corners of her mouth.

"Oh, David could be a heel, no doubt about it. But Amber always forgave him. I think she knew how he was and had learned to live with it."

"Any of those women in there likely candidates?"

"You mean did any of them sleep with David?"

"Uh-huh."

She glanced over her shoulder, inventoried the room.

"Not that I know of. Those are mostly Amber's friends. Some of them barely knew David. But you never know what the old boy might've had going on the side."

I wanted to ask Etta directly whether *she'd* ever entertained the old boy, but I didn't have the guts. She smiled again, probably reading my mind, then glanced over toward the widow.

"Amber seems to be holding up a little better," she said. "Maybe you could have your talk with her now."

"Good idea." I'd barely touched the food, but I tossed the plate in the trash under the sink and edged toward the living room. Etta Dangler cut me off, planting her scrumptious self in the doorway.

"If you need me for anything, sugar, you just call."

"Um, right. Thank you."

She allowed me to pass, but only by inches, and I got another whiff of her and felt the heat from her body. Gulp.

Amber's friends gave me hard looks as I approached, but I smiled them off and squatted in front of her.

"Mrs. Field? You feel up to a quick business conversation?"

Amber looked at me with dead eyes. But something finally flickered in there and she nodded.

"Where can we have some privacy?"

She pointed off toward the far end of the house, and I followed her to a bedroom decorated with Shaker furniture and ruffly pillows. She perched on the edge of the bed, and I dragged over a straight-backed chair and sat directly in front of her.

"How are you holding up?"

She shrugged, sighed. All the well-wishers in the other room hadn't done much for her mood.

"I need a couple of things from you; then I'll be on my way. You should rest."

She nodded wearily.

"First, Anna Lipscomb over at the Biology Department wouldn't let me in David's office."

I saw a spark there, the briefest of fires, at the mention of Lipscomb's name. Then it vanished.

"I think it'll help my investigation," I continued, "if I can look around, maybe go through David's files."

"I'll call her." Amber's voice sounded as if she'd been drinking sand. "I've got a key. You can go in there whenever you like."

"Thanks."

Amber raised an eyebrow, silently asking the question, What else? This would be the sticky part, I knew.

"I don't know quite how to ask the other question," I

said. "Some people I talked to indicated that David might've, well, maybe it's just gossip, I don't know—"

"What did they say?" The flame definitely burned in her eyes now. Something wild there, too, like you see when a horse goes galloping out of control. I leaned back in my chair, gave her some room. I didn't want to be trampled.

"Just that maybe David had, um, seen other women since you two were married."

"Affairs? They said David had affairs?"

"Well, nobody came right out—"

"Who said this?" Her voice went low, scary. "I'll kill them before I let them talk about David like that."

"Now, Mrs. Field, let's not get too riled up—"

"The lying bastards. They're jealous! All of them! My husband was a brilliant, brilliant man. The rest of them are mental midgets compared with him. They just can't stand it. Why, I'll—"

"Mrs. Field!" I grasped her flailing hand. "Take it easy. It's just gossip. It can't hurt him. It can't hurt you. I shouldn't even have brought it up."

She trembled with anger and grief. "Then why did you?"

"I have to look at every possibility. If the gossip is true, then an illicit lover could be a suspect. You see that, don't you?"

The quaking subsided a little. Amber cleared her throat, took deep breaths.

"I'm sorry, Mr. Mabry. I'm just…I'm just so tired."

"I know. You should rest. Do you want me to run off your friends so you can sleep?"

She nodded gratefully, fell back on the bed, and scooted up to clutch a pillow.

She told me where to find the office key ring in a little jar on the dresser; then I said good-bye and went into the living room to ease out Amber's supportive friends. Most seemed relieved to hear Amber needed a nap and that they were free to go. I held the door open for them amid a general bustle of snapping purses and clicking heels and kiss-kiss farewells. Etta Dangler was the last to reach the door, and she spun on me and stood too close and licked her lips.

"It was nice meeting you, Bubba."

"Same here. Bye now."

"You in a hurry? Maybe we could talk some more. Amber wouldn't mind."

I glanced at my wristwatch, remembered who I was, where I was supposed to be.

"In fact, I *am* in a hurry. I'm late for a tuxedo fitting."

"Tuxedo? Aren't we uptown? What do you need with a monkey suit?"

"I'm getting married. Week from tomorrow."

The distance between us grew ever so slightly. I thought I felt a chill, but Etta cocked her head, looked up me, almost smiling.

"Getting married? Who's the lucky girl?"

"Her name's Felicia. Newspaper reporter. You wouldn't know her."

God, I hoped that was true. If Felicia knew I had even talked to a flirt monster like Etta Dangler, she'd have my balls—

"Week from tomorrow, huh? Well, a lot can happen in a week. You nervous yet?"

"I'm always nervous."

"Well, if you need anything, feel free to call me. I'm in the book."

I was thinking, I'll bet you are. Probably in the Yellow Pages under "Man-eater."

"With your investigation, I mean. I knew David pretty well. Maybe I can help."

I found my voice, thanked her, edged toward the door.

"Walk me out?"

"Sure. But I really am in a hurry."

"Okay." She gave me that smile again. "I'm ready. Don't get your shorts in a knot."

She walked in a languid, long-legged, hip-swinging fashion that dreams are made of. Not like Felicia, who always looks like she could break into a run any second. I tried not to watch, but it was like turning away from a train wreck. Some things are too riveting.

"So long, Bubba." She opened the door of a little beetle green Japanese convertible, tossed her hair, cranked the engine.

I waved, turned, hurried away. I didn't want to see her drive off, that red mane flying in the wind. I'd look foolish running down the street after her.

SEVEN

THE FORMAL-WEAR PLACE was just east of the university, among a strip of bridal shops that occupied three blocks of Central Avenue. The tiny guy behind the counter made a point of looking at his watch as I blew through the door fifteen minutes late.

I have this private theory about evolution. People didn't just evolve from apes, but from all sorts of animals. We've all seen people with horsey faces or hangdog expressions or popped eyes like a goldfish. And there are more than a few snakes walking around on two legs, mostly in the legal profession. Take some of the people I'd met lately. Amber Field had the loyal eyes and earnest nervousness of a beagle. Etta Dangler's ancestors were some sort of sleek panthers. Doc Slagg, with his gray bristles and light blue eyes, evolved from a wolf. Emil Pugh? I'm not sure, maybe a maggot. And me? I ain't nothing but a hound dawg.

The little swish behind the counter at the tux shop had been a pussycat in a previous life, no question. He slinked around the end of the counter, twitching his tail, looking smug. He practically rubbed against my legs, purring.

"I am José," he announced. "You must be Mr. Mabry."

"That's right. And I'm in a hurry. Let's get this over with."

I hate cats.

''Tut-tut, Mr. Mabry, we mustn't rush. You want to look splendid on your wedding day.''

''No problem. I'm a perfect forty-two long. Write it up and let me out of here.''

The place gave me the heebies. Headless mannequins dressed to the nines stood around the room as if engaged in a bizarre cocktail party. One whole wall was covered by shiny plastic boxes full of flashy cummerbunds and bow ties. Behind the counter hung two rows of tuxedos ready to go, covered in Saran Wrap and labeled with the names of their victims—I mean, customers.

Felicia had insisted on the tuxedo. She wanted our wedding day to be a storybook affair, from her virginal white gown to the three-tiered cake. ''We're only going to do this once,'' she'd said, ''so we might as well go whole hog.'' It's a wonder she didn't ask me to turn a pumpkin into a coach for the ride to the chapel.

I'd won at least one point in our debate—no fancy colors or frills on my tux, basic black. Pleated shirt, shiny shoes. It should've been the kind of order you could call in, but José had insisted that I keep the appointment to be measured. I think he just liked to get close to guys with his measuring tape.

I hadn't worn a tuxedo since the high school prom, nearly two decades ago. No event since had required one, and I probably would've avoided such an occasion if one had arisen. I'd just as soon drape myself in silverware as formal wear.

I'd gone with basic black for the prom, too, though it was an era—the late seventies—when guys thought it was cool to wear powder blue polyester tuxes or something in emerald crushed velvet. My date, Linda Sue Bolivar, had understood my haberdashery hesitation, though she had shown none of it herself. She'd worn a filmy yellow gown that set off her black hair and creamy shoulders. You wouldn't think such an insubstantial piece of clothing would've been difficult to remove, but Linda Sue had managed to keep her dress on all night, while all around us other prom couples were getting naked and rocking cars and getting pregnant.

I was lucky to have a date at all. If Linda Sue hadn't broke up with Butchie Miller, her longtime boyfriend, a couple of weeks before the prom, I'd have been watching the whole affair from the town pool hall. My family was something of a laughingstock in Nazareth, Mississippi. Linda Sue risked her own place in teenage society by being seen with me, but I guess she thought it was better than missing the prom altogether.

I don't know whatever happened to Linda Sue Bolivar, and I don't keep close track of my family back in Mississippi. I hadn't even told any of them about the wedding. Felicia initially pestered me to invite them, but she understood my history and why having my mother praying in the chapel would make me even more nervous.

My mother, Eloise Cutwaller Mabry, is something of a religious fanatic. No, that's an understatement. My mother may be this country's premiere religious fanatic. When I was a kid, she invited Jesus Christ into our home. Nothing wrong with that, you might think, but I'm not being figurative here. My mother's Jesus turned out to be some drug-addled hippie who lived in the piney woods near our country home. My mother still clung to the belief that it really was Christ, and tabloid newspapers still occasionally had great fun reporting about her.

A generation earlier, my maternal grandfather, Pincus Cutwaller, took a header out of the Waldorf-Astoria in New York when he heard about the Martian invasion on radio's "War of the Worlds"—the only casualty in a fictional war.

I hadn't even been alive for that embarrassment, but I suffered the Cutwaller taint. The most gullible family in Mississippi, bar none. They don't forget things like that in a small town in the South.

Of course, I couldn't just move west and lay low and hope the Cutwaller gullibility gene would skip a generation. I'd had my own run-in with infamy. Couple of years ago, a client entered my life who appeared to be the living Elvis Presley. Oh, sure, you're thinking, Elvis keeps turning up in convenience stores and Laundromats. But this guy sure seemed to be the real deal. If he was an impostor, he was using the resemblance to his advantage. Oh, never mind. I don't like to recall the ridicule. I let Felicia talk me into writing a book about the adventure, against my better judgment, and pretty soon everyone knew about it. I still occasionally run into somebody who remembers the Elvis business and insists on talking about it.

You'd think such an experience would've sharpened me. But people still fooled me, or talked me into things I didn't want to do. Look at me now, for instance, being measured by the Fruit of the Loom for a tuxedo I didn't even want to wear.

For that matter, how could I be sure getting married was the right thing to do? Sure, I initiated the whole thing, but how did I know Felicia hadn't somehow subtly steered me to the decision? She certainly knew how to play me. Was I being a sucker in taking the Big Step with someone as perpetually pushy as Felicia?

Having Etta Dangler make a run at me didn't help. If I could get so easily aroused, could be made so instantly stupid, was I really ready to settle down with one woman? I didn't want to end up like David Field, chasing skirts, running from one affair to another. I might be a gullible goof, but I stick to my promises. And what was a marriage, really, but the biggest of promises, made in front of God and everybody?

The part I understood least of all: Why was it necessary to get gussied up in evening wear to make such a promise?

"Okay, now we do the inseam," said José, who'd already measured my chest, arms, and waist (where had that new inch there come from?). He dropped to his knees in front of me, held one end of the tape measure to my ankle, started reaching up with the other hand.

"I'll take care of this end," I said, taking the tape from him and holding it to my crotch.

José smiled, winked at me. I resisted the urge to wrap the tape measure very tightly around his neck.

When we finished, I paid my deposit, wrote down the time I was supposed to pick up the tux, and hustled out of there. José meowed his good-byes as the door jangled shut behind me.

I drove the long way back to Felicia's apartment, letting the Ram meander up the Cruise while I took in the sights: hookers dealing blow jobs from the corner by Pussycat Erotic Videos; an emaciated black woman named Idabelle, pushing her shopping cart full of junk, muttering to herself; a scammer named Gus McCoy, talking fast to some tourist in Bermuda shorts, probably pushing some scheme that would result in the vacation money in Gus's pocket and the tourist standing by his Winnebago, scratching his head.

Ah, the Cruise. I missed it. Living there, among the criminals and crazies, had kept me on my toes. You can't be naïve and survive there for long, but I'd done it for a decade. I wondered if I'd lose that edge now that I'd moved to the Heights. An old married man, that's what I'd become, moldering at home in my reclining chair, unaware of the scams and the scrapes the cold, cruel world could offer.

EIGHT

FELICIA GOT HOME NOT LONG after I arrived. I'd turned on a college football game, settled down with a beer, but it quickly became clear that the game, for me, was over. Felicia stood between me and the TV, talking about her idiot editor, who'd called her to the office when she really needed to be spending time with Denise and finalizing the gift list. After five minutes of this, I turned the television off.

"What was so important they had to call you in on a Saturday?"

My expression of interest threw her off. She'd grown accustomed to talking without me actually listening. We were perfect for each other.

"What?"

"What was it they wanted?"

"Oh, that. Actually, it might be pretty good. Maybe not worth ruining my Saturday, but pretty good. This old Navajo guy says his land was stolen."

"Out by the Rio Puerco?"

"Yeah. How did you know that?"

"That's what you've been writing about, right?"

She beamed. Reporters think nobody notices their by-lines, but I watch for Felicia's. I've learned over the past couple of years. Gonna read the paper anyway, might as well pay attention and score a few points.

"They're all coming out of the woodwork because they're reading about it in the *Gazette*," I continued. "First, there was Amber Field, the lady you sent to me, thank you very much. Now, there's this Indian. What's his name?"

"Harry Whitewoman."

"What?"

"I know. I didn't believe it either. I thought he was making fun of me. I made him show me his driver's license."

"How'd he react to that?"

"Okay. I think he's used to it. Anyway, I may be onto something with him."

"Sit down and tell me about it."

Another expression of interest. I was racking up the points here. Maybe I could keep the conversation steered for the whole evening. No more Denise or the bridal registry or my tuxedo.

Grinning, Felicia flopped onto the sofa opposite me, pulled a pack of Virginia Slims from her shirt pocket, lit one up. She didn't seem to notice I'd emptied the ashtray next to her, so no points there, but what the hell, I was on a roll. I didn't need 'em.

"Okay," she began, "so you've been reading the stories about the Rio Puerco development?"

"Most of them."

"Then you know this Rio Rancho bunch called Tierra Verde is on the verge of announcing a series of planned communities there."

Actually, I had no recollection of anything called Tierra Verde, but I nodded and grunted knowingly.

"Tierra Verde is relatively new on the scene, and most of that land has been tied up for decades by other companies, all these vultures waiting for the right time to swoop down on the land boom. So, how did Tierra Verde suddenly get all this land out there?"

I shrugged.

"That's what I've been trying to find out. I've gone through the county records a dozen times. Everything looks on the up-and-up. Nobody wants to say anything bad about Tierra Verde. But there's a bad smell there. I've just got to keep digging."

"What do you *think* they're up to?"

"I'm getting to that. How come everybody's suddenly willing to sell their land now, just when it looks like the boom is finally really going to happen? That's the question. Now, Harry Whitewoman comes into my life."

"I can't believe that's his real name."

"It is, trust me. So along comes Harry Whitewoman, who has swallowed his fear and approached the newspaper with his story. Seems Harry owned a little over a hundred acres out between the Rio Puerco and the edge of the Canoncito Navajo reservation. You know where that is?"

"West of town someplace."

"Right. Anyway, it's right in the way, see? If somebody wants to push roads through that empty country out there and build houses and stores and schools, it's all gotta go through Whitewoman's land."

"So they asked him to sell it."

"No, they didn't *ask* him. Couple of goons came around and insisted he hand over the deed at bargain-basement rates. Harry says no thanks. Then his favorite dog turns up dead. All the tires on his truck go flat. He finds rattlesnakes in his house."

"All within a short period of time?"

"You got it. Then the goons come around again, make him a little sweeter offer, make it clear more bad things will happen if he doesn't accept."

"So Harry goes to the newspaper."

"No. Harry sells them the land. He was too scared. And

he's poor. And he's got a little drinking problem. Anyway, he signs over the deed, takes the money, and goes back to the reservation.''

"That's where his house is?"

"Right. He lives on Indian land, not the private parcel. It was just for grazing a few sheep, see? No big loss to him. But then he gets back to the Canoncito reservation and tells his buddies what he's done, and they tell him he's crazy, that the land is worth a fortune now. Harry starts to have second thoughts. Maybe he should've stood up to the goons, demanded more. Maybe he got screwed.''

"So *then* Harry goes to the newspaper."

"Right. And it just happened to be on a Saturday."

"Did you write a story for tomorrow's paper?"

"No. I couldn't reach anybody at Tierra Verde. They'll just deny it anyway, but I've gotta give them a chance to comment."

"Couldn't you call the owner at home?"

"Nobody at Tierra Verde gives out their home number, except their 'spokesman,' a slimy guy named Sammy Flick, and he wasn't home today. The person I really want to interview is the owner of the company, a mystery man named Tommy Greene."

"Mystery man? Aren't we being a little dramatic?"

Felicia ticked off her points on her fingers.

"He won't meet the press. I can't find anybody who's ever met him face-to-face. Everybody seems scared of him. And, apparently, he has goons who frighten old Indian men."

I scratched my chin, thought over what she'd said.

"Well, other than the scaring little old men part, what do you think this Tommy Greene has to hide?"

"I don't know. I think maybe the whole land deal's some kinda scam. *Tierra verde* indeed."

Felicia snorted, stubbed out her cigarette, flopped back on the sofa. My Spanish is weak, but even I know what *verde* means, and there is nothing green about the land out by the Rio Puerco.

"It's like the Vikings," she said, her voice dripping disgust.

"Whoa, you lost me there."

"Don't you know about Greenland? Didn't they teach you anything in school in Mississippi?"

"They taught us the words to 'Dixie.' 'Wish I was in the land of cotton—'"

Felicia rolled her eyes.

"Thousand years ago, some Viking—I think it was Erik the Red, one of those guys—discovered Greenland. So he goes back to Denmark or Sweden or wherever he was from to tell everybody about this new real estate he'd uncovered."

"I'm with you so far."

"He had to think up a name for this giant island, something that would lure settlers there. So he called it Greenland, even though it was a miserable chunk of ice with nothing green about it."

"And that's what Tommy Greene is doing with the Rio Puerco?"

"Looks like it to me. Why would anyone with their eyes open want to live out there?"

"Maybe the houses will be affordable. Albuquerque could use that."

"Maybe, but you'd spend on gasoline driving back and forth into the city what you'd save in rent. And where are they going to get water out there? Where will they shop?"

I leaned forward, rested my elbows on my knees, cracked a few knuckles. I'd scored so many points, I hated to lose any by bringing up the obvious.

"Hon, isn't it possible the man called his company Tierra Verde because his *name* is Greene?"

She glowered at me.

"Don't you think I've thought of that already?"

"I couldn't tell. You made him sound like this Viking—"

"Oh, never mind. I'm tired of thinking about this land deal anyway. What I need to be working on is the wedding."

Dang. I thought I had her going.

"Speaking of green, I started having second thoughts about that green pattern for the everyday china. I brought the brochure home. Let me just get it out of my purse. I want you to look it over with me."

I looked longingly at the TV's remote control.

NINE

THE NEXT DAY, FELICIA AND I had a leisurely morning over a pot of coffee and the six-pound Sunday *Gazette* before we went our separate ways. She zoomed off to the newsroom to make more attempts at shaking something loose from Tierra Verde officials. I drove to the university for a little breaking and entering.

Okay, so I had permission and I had keys. But sneaking into the empty Biology Department building on a Sunday still felt criminal. What if Amber Field had forgotten to call Anna Lipscomb and give her my clearance? Suppose Lipscomb hadn't bothered to mention this to anyone like, say, the university police? That'd be just what I needed, a hassle from some rent-a-cop with poor vision and an itchy trigger finger.

The parking lots were nearly empty, but I still parked at a meter two blocks away from the building so I wouldn't draw any attention. Then I skulked along the sidewalk, David Field's keys feeling hot in my hand.

No need for sneaking, as it turned out. The campus was practically empty. Just a young couple on Rollerblades whizzing past, their skates clicking over the joints in the sidewalk. Somebody's German shepherd running loose, its tongue hanging out the side of its mouth, not the slightest bit interested in me.

I made my way to the front doors of the building, hung

around a cactus garden, trying to look as if I wasn't about
to go where I didn't belong. Just another nature lover studying the spiny cacti. Nobody in sight. I stole over to the
glass doors. Locked.

David Field had been thoughtful enough to label the
dozen or so keys on the ring, and I searched through them
until I located one marked "Back Door." I slunk around
the building until I found a door cut into the stucco wall.
I tried the key. *Click,* I was inside.

The hallway was dark, but lights shone at either end—
enough for me to make out the names on the office doors.
I went down one hallway and up another before I found
Field's office. Another search through the labeled keys, another click in the lock, and I was in the late biologist's
office.

I left the door open, flicked on the overhead light, and
looked around. Unlike other offices I'd seen on campus,
Field's was clean and orderly. A floor-to-ceiling bookshelf
filled one wall and a couple of file cabinets leaned against
another. The bookshelf was jammed full, books lined up
neatly, interrupted only by a stuffed hawk of some kind,
wings spread, glaring down at me with fierce eyes. Probably the work of Emil Pugh. I suppressed a shudder.

In the center of the windowless room stood Field's desk,
the desktop cleared except for a blotter, a clock, a couple
of pens. Tidy. No papers lying out anywhere. No note that
said, "Look for my body out in the desert" or "They're
trying to kill me."

I've never had a desk of my own, except for the flimsy
all-in-ones we had in school. I wondered what such a clean
desk indicated about Field, what it should tell me about his
personality. Organization is not my specialty. If I did have
a desk, it probably would look like a landfill.

I felt uneasy about being in the dead man's space. I took

deep breaths, edged around the corner of the desk, sat in David Field's chair. The chair was an old-fashioned swiveler, oak with curved arms, not especially comfortable, but familiar somehow. Field probably didn't spend much time sitting anyway. He probably hung off the end of his pristine desk, doing sit-ups while reciting Milton. Renaissance man. Muscles and tan and brains. Usually, I get some empathy for the person I'm hunting in a missing-person case. And, in a murder case, it's probably important to get inside the head of the victim. But David Field seemed too perfect to be approachable, his only flaw an overly strong libido. I had no idea, really, what kind of man he was, what secrets he kept hidden.

I sighed. Maybe searching his office would turn up something. I found the tiny key to his desk on my ring, unlocked the wide center drawer.

The usual pens and paper clips and Post-its, all properly compartmentalized. A couple of file folders full of departmental memos, Anna Lipscomb's name signed at the bottom of each. She wrote with the same stiff formality that she used in speech. No surprises there. Then another file, under the others, full of what looked like field notes. I tried to decipher them, but they were full of Latin and numbers and they made me dizzy. There was one interesting item at the back of the folder, though: a color photograph, a close-up shot of one of those pushy little owls I'd seen at the murder scene. Could the owls be what he was researching? Good possibility. Nothing else moving out there. I set the folder aside for further study.

I searched through the other drawers in the desk and came up empty. No provocative love letters, no threats, no receipts for some no-tell motel. Nada.

I stood, stretched, moved to the file cabinets, began to give them the same treatment. Most of the folders were full of typewritten studies and research reports indecipherable to the quick glance. I was elbow-deep in the second drawer when a voice startled the hell out of me.

"What do you think you're doing?"

I jumped, hit my funny bone on the corner of the drawer, did a little ooch-ouch dance around the room. I turned, to find a woman standing in the doorway, arms akimbo, glaring at me. She looked sturdy in her safari shorts and cotton shirt, deeply tanned and well muscled. Sort of a female version of David Field. She had a big square face and sun-bleached hair and she looked ready to plant one of her bulky hiking boots right up my ass.

"Oh, hi. Ow. Uh, I'm a private detective. I've got permission to be here."

"Is that so? From whom?"

Whom—not so angry as to lose her grammar.

"Amber Field."

She harrumphed, said, "You're not mixing up those files, are you?"

"No, I'm very careful. Hey, wait a minute. Why am I explaining myself to you? Who are you?"

"My name's Liz Weston. I work here."

I let go of my throbbing elbow long enough to shake her hand.

"Bubba Mabry. Mrs. Field hired me to investigate her husband's death."

"Murder, you mean."

"Yeah, right. Murder. It's not like he shot himself in the back."

She blanched a little.

"Sorry. Were you friends with David Field?"

"We worked together for several years."

"You're a biologist, too?"

"Ornithologist."

"Ornery what?"

"Ornithologist. I study birds. David's research and mine sometimes overlapped."

"I thought he didn't collaborate with anybody."

She lifted a shoulder, sighed. "No, he didn't. Not really. Not even with me."

"So you don't know what he was doing out there where he got killed?"

"No. Nobody seems to know."

"Yeah, that's what I keep finding, too."

"You talked to people in the department?"

"A few. On Friday. I didn't see you around."

"I just returned from the Four Corners area. I've been out in the field for three weeks."

That explained the tan and the hair. She looked baked from all sides.

"Did you just hear about Field?"

She shook her head, chewed on her lower lip.

"I read about it in the Farmington newspaper. It made the front page, even up there."

"You got any idea who might've killed him?"

She shook her head silently, but I could tell she was thinking. I waited. Sometimes, saying nothing will get people to talk because silence makes them uncomfortable. Other times, they'll just think I'm an idiot and wander off. I couldn't tell which way it would go with Liz Weston.

"The article," she began, "said he was doing research out there. It hinted that might've been the reason somebody killed him, but that doesn't make any sense. Who cares what we do in the field?"

"Maybe it was something personal," I ventured. "Field have any enemies?"

She shrugged. "Who doesn't? But I can't think of anyone who'd want to kill him."

The next question would take me onto thin ice, but I bravely skated on out there.

"Some people told me David liked to flirt with the coeds. You know anything about that?"

She gave me a sharp look and her arms crossed over her chest defensively. Didn't need to be a body-language expert to see I'd struck a nerve.

"David might've had his little adventures, but he was careful," she said. "It's not like he was diddling house-wives and some jealous husband tracked him down."

"You know who he was 'diddling'?"

She shook her head, pressed her lips together so no words could escape.

"I don't think I want to have this conversation," she said finally. "I'm tired and I need a shower, and I don't need this. David's gone and I'm sorry, but I won't want to muck around in his life right now."

I nodded my understanding.

"Finish what you were doing," she said, "but don't mess up those files. At some point, somebody—probably me—will have to go through them and decipher what David left behind."

I told her I'd be careful, and she turned with a sigh and strode off down the hall. I waited there a minute, ready for somebody else to pop through the doorway, then turned back to my fruitless search through Field's files.

An hour later, I was done. I'd turned up exactly nothing. I cleaned up behind myself, tucked the owl folder under my arm, and left by the back door.

It occurred to me as I reached the truck that I should've asked Liz Weston about the owls, see what an ornithologist would make of the notes. Maybe she could've told me whether there was any reason for Field to study them. But turning back would mean going again into that spooky, empty building, and I probably wouldn't find her anyway. She said she was going home for a shower. I made a mental note to talk to her again, whether either of us liked it or not.

TEN

I WAS HEADED HOME, but I got an idea and stopped at a pay phone instead. The dispatcher who answered the call said Lieutenant Erndow was in his office but was on the phone. She asked if I wanted to leave a message. I told her no thanks and hung up. Then I cranked up the Ram and turned back the way I'd come, driving toward downtown.

Naturally, not even driving to the sheriff's department could be easy on a day like this. Some festival was under way on Civic Plaza, and orange sawhorses blocked off the streets. Since the cop shop was on the far side of the plaza, the blockade meant I had to drive around and around the one-way streets, searching for a place to park the truck.

What somebody needs to invent is a fold-up car. You'd drive it somewhere, then fold it down into the size of a briefcase and just carry it along with you. No parking problems ever again. Of course, a vehicle the size of the Ram would be a load to carry. It's certainly a pain to park. Finally, I found an empty space in a gravel lot three blocks north of police headquarters and trudged south, shaking my head and grumbling.

I could hear the music of a brass band clanging from the plaza, so I steered clear of the crowds there. Albuquerque's so starved for entertainment, people will turn out for anything.

Down the block, a cluster of women stood on the sidewalk, their heads craned skyward, gesturing with their hands in strange signals, as if they were guiding a UFO to earth. I looked up to see what they were staring at, and I nearly tripped over a crack in the sidewalk. Then I recognized what was happening. The nearest building was the county jail, seven stories of misery broken by windows too narrow for anyone to slip through. Orange-jumpsuited inmates pressed against the skinny windows on the upper floors, sending messages to the women with similar sign language. I'd heard about this weird form of communication from the cons I knew. It was a way to see your squeeze and get some messages across without waiting for visitation hours. I couldn't understand anything they were saying to one another, wondered whether each couple had their own code, whether illegalities were being discussed or whether it was all just sex talk.

One of the women, who wore her henna hair sprayed tall and rigid, glanced over at me, looked around like she was up to something. I averted my eyes, cut them back to her just in time to see her grab the hem of her black blouse and lift it over her face, exposing pendulous brown-tipped breasts. Then she quickly lowered her shirt, blushing slightly, smiling. I looked up, to see the inmates miming applause. Now, that's entertainment.

I jaywalked across Roma Avenue to the cop shop, savored the blast of refrigerated air as I opened the door. An APD uniform sat at a reception desk just inside, and I lied to him, saying I had an appointment with Erndow. He checked a sign-in sheet, saw that Erndow was still in the building, then gave me a visitor's badge and directions to the lieutenant's office.

Nobody paid me any attention as I got off the elevator and strolled into the sheriff's department. Deputies sat at desks here and there, some in their weekend T-shirts, typing up overdue reports. I walked past them without a word, spotted the frosted glass office that held Erndow, knocked on his door.

Erndow sat behind his desk, erect and rigid as a hard-on, looking over some paperwork.

"What are you doing here?"

A fine greeting.

"Seemed like we're covering the same ground. Thought we could compare notes."

"Excuse me?" It was said with just enough indignation to remind me who was the real investigator here—as if I needed reminding. Erndow watched me with unnerving, nearly colorless gray eyes. His shiny head reflected the overhead lights.

"Let me rephrase that. Amber Field has asked me to stay on the case, and I wondered if I could help you in any way."

Erndow's jaw unclenched ever so slightly, so I guess I'd said the right thing.

"I was just looking over the autopsy report on David Field," he said.

The mention of that report made my hand itch. I scratched it mindlessly, thinking how badly I needed to know what was on that paper.

"Looks the same on paper as it did out in the field," he said grimly. "One shot in the back, two in the back of the head. Twenty-two-caliber. Whoever did this knew what he was doing."

"Quick and easy."

"That's right. You got any ideas who it might've been?"

"None. I get the impression David Field wasn't the easiest guy to like, but nobody's said they considered killing him."

Erndow nodded silently. I noticed the nameplate on his

desk: LT. CLORIS ERNDOW. Cloris? Whew. No wonder he's such a sourpuss.

"The coroner also had plenty to say about how somebody had puked all over the evidence."

Ouch. That embarrassment had managed to slip my mind. My cheeks warmed.

"I'm really sorry about that. Hope it didn't ruin your case."

He shook his head.

"Don't seem to have much of a case anyway. No witnesses, no tire tracks, no footprints. Whoever killed that man slipped in, popped him, covered him up with that little tent, and vanished."

"You're saying it was a professional job?"

"I don't remember those words slipping through my lips."

I was thinking, What lips? But I said, "That's what it sounds like to me."

"It does, huh? And you have lots of experience with murder investigations?"

"I read a lot."

Erndow grunted, then went back to looking at his papers, as if he expected me to dry up and blow away. Maybe I would.

"I talked to some of the same people you did over at the Biology Department," I said.

"Is that so? And nobody confessed, huh?"

"Nah. They just hinted a lot about what a heel the late Mr. Field could be."

He gave me a curt nod.

"You know, Mabry, I'd appreciate it if you didn't talk to my witnesses. This is a murder investigation, and we don't need some amateur sticking his dick in things and stirring them up."

"I'll be careful not to interfere."

"See that you do."

I turned to leave. I clearly wasn't getting anywhere here.

"Besides," he said before I could get to the door, "you're probably working for the number-one suspect."

"What?"

"Amber Field. I think she's at the top of the list, don't you?"

I hadn't thought that for a moment, but I said, "Yeah, that occurred to me. But she seems awfully broken up over his death to be the killer."

"That's natural. Or a very good act."

"What makes you think she did it?"

"I'm not saying she did. But she had motive. Everybody says Field was sleeping around on her. These days, with all the diseases out there, that can be deadly. She had opportunity. She's the only one who seems to have known Field was out in that particular region of the outback."

"What about method?" I asked, showing him I knew the third leg of this stool.

"A twenty-two? You can get them anywhere, easy as buying a hamburger. And they're easily disposed of. I imagine that gun's at the bottom of the Rio Grande by now."

I still stood with my hand on the doorknob. Amber Field? Couldn't be. I thought about how angry she got when I mentioned the gossip, how she stood by her man, even unto death. No, Erndow was wrong. It wasn't Amber.

"And what about you, Mabry? Where do you fit into all of this?"

"What do you mean?"

"Mrs. Field hired you when again? The day before you found the body? Sure it wasn't a couple of days earlier, maybe she needed somebody to pull the trigger for her?"

"Now, hold on a minute—"

"How did she get your name?"

I thought about Felicia, her recommending me to Amber Field. I didn't want to drag my betrothed into this mess. Plus, I didn't want to mention the newspaper connection. More media attention Erndow didn't need. It might affect his perfect posture.

"I don't know. Guess she found me in the Yellow Pages."

Erndow nearly smiled.

"I'd better go," I said.

"One more thing." He didn't raise his voice, but it was enough to stall me in the doorway, keep me from running, which is what my feet wanted to do.

"Tell Mrs. Field the coroner has released the body and the funeral home can pick it up. I understand the funeral's set for Wednesday."

"Is that so? I didn't know that."

"You didn't?"

"Hell, Lieutenant, I don't know anything anymore."

ELEVEN

FELICIA'S BATTERED BROWN Toyota was parked in her space at the apartment complex. I found myself bracing for whatever new wedding-related predicament she'd cooked up. That's not the way coming home should feel. I mean, I'm not expecting some sort of "Luuu-cey, I'm ho-ome!" perfect sitcom life. But home should be about love and comfort and warmth, not anxiety and misgivings. God, I'd be glad when the wedding was over. Sure, I trembled at the thought of saying those vows, but at least they'd mark the end of all the planning and the beginning of something completely different.

I swung open the door and peeked inside, to see Felicia bent over the dining room table, her head on her hands, including one that held a smoldering cigarette in dangerous proximity to her hair. She was studying a large paper that covered the top of the table, and I dreaded to think what part of the wedding that giant chart might entail.

"Hi, I'm home."

She grunted a hello without looking up. I eased over toward her, looking at the paper, finally making it out to be a map. Wincing, I asked, "So, are we adding real estate to the gift list?"

"What?" She finally looked up, saw it was me standing there.

"The map, what's it for?"

"Oh, this." She straightened, stubbed out the smoke, leaned back in her chair. "This shows all the land out by the Rio Puerco."

"Really?" I might be able to use that. "Where'd you get it?"

"At the office. We keep all these on file."

"And you just took it?"

"Yeah. So? They've got others."

I pulled out a chair, sat down beside her.

"So whatcha looking for?"

"I was trying to figure out where you found David Field's body."

"Yeah? Guess I got here just in time."

"Think you can find it?"

"Let me look." I located Rio Rancho and the Rio Puerco and pointed at the space between. "Somewhere in here. About there."

She nodded, barely looking at the point I was showing with a finger.

"That's what I thought."

She lit another cigarette, puffed the smoke toward the ceiling.

"Well, if you already knew, then why did you bother to ask?"

Why was she so grumpy? I'd just as soon talk about the bridal registry as put up with this.

"Guess what's about to happen on that spot."

"Huh?"

"Okay, genius detective, listen. Today, I had to work, right?"

"Yeah."

"And I told you what it was about, right?"

I had no recollection of this.

"Right."

"Now I'm sitting here, looking at this map for David Field's corpse. What does your mighty deductive reasoning make of that?"

Not much. I strained my brain, trying to see the connection she was getting at, but all I got was the beginnings of a headache.

"Is that on Harry Whitewoman's land?"

"No, no. His land is over here." She pointed south and west of the spot where I still had my finger pegged to the map.

"Then I don't get it."

She shook her head.

"Look, Sherlock, I was going to a Tierra Verde press conference today, right?"

That's right. That's what she'd said over coffee that morning. I'd been reading the sports page.

"Right."

"As expected, Tierra Verde's sweaty little flack announced they were breaking ground on their new planned community southwest of Rio Rancho."

"Okay."

"This whole area"—she pushed my hand out of the way, made a big circle around the indentation I'd left in the map—"will become Tierra Verde's first big project, whole neighborhoods and a shopping center and roads going in and out. They're calling it Tierra Oeste. So now you see."

I didn't see dick. What was she getting at? David Field was killed in a big old wasteland of sand and sagebrush that soon would become a big old wasteland of stucco suburbs. So?

I caught Felicia looking at me. It felt like she was studying my face for any sign of life, as if she were looking in my brain to see whether any gears were turning in there. I hated to disappoint her.

"David Field was killed right where they want to put the new development," she said, speaking slowing and clearly, the way you'd try to impart information to an idiot. "Maybe he was in somebody's way."

Oh. Why didn't she just say so? Why prove that I'm stupid first? Is that any way for a soon-to-be-blushing-bride to act?

"It wasn't like he was squatting out there," I said. "If he was in the way, they could've just waited for him to go home."

She shrugged, smushed out the new cigarette half-smoked.

"Maybe so. But maybe he knew something that would screw up their plans."

"Like what?"

"I don't know. But you'd better watch yourself if you're going to poke around in Field's death. Remember what the Tierra Verde boys did to Harry Whitewoman."

"I'm not a doddering old Indian."

"You're not Mike Hammer, either. Just be careful."

"What about you? You're the one who's trying to expose Tierra Verde at every turn, trying to find conspiracies. Hell, now you're even trying to link them to murder. You're the one who ought to be careful."

"They don't scare me." She had that set to her jaw, that glitter in her eyes, and I knew it was true. Something sort of arousing about such ferocity, as long as it's not directed at you.

"I'm sure they don't, hon," I said, patting her arm. "But I don't think you've scared *them* yet, either. They're going ahead with their plans."

"Yeah," she said, sounding glum.

"Hey, speaking of Harry Whitewoman, did you ask the Tierra Verde people about his story?"

"Sammy Flick, the little weasel, acted like he'd never heard of Harry. Said he'd look into it. Right."

"The paper still going to run the story?"

"Not so far. The editors are all chickenshit. Who are they going to believe, the 'doddering old Indian' or a big corporation that's got more lawyers than Jimmy Carter's got teeth?"

"What about Tommy Greene? Anything on him?"

"Flick the Flack says Greene is, quote, 'a very private person.' You can say that again. Nobody even knows what the bastard looks like, much less where he got his money. The whole thing's driving me crazy."

Felicia got up from the table, stretched her arms widely, arched her back. Her loose camp shirt rode up, exposing an inch of creamy belly. I felt something go *boing* in my groin.

"Maybe you're working too hard. You need to do something to take your mind off Tierra Verde and the wedding and everything."

She dropped her arms, gave me the once-over.

"What did you have in mind?"

"How about we play a game? We'll turn out all the lights, take off our clothes, and see which of us can make the other one squeal first."

She looked dubious, wary. Uh-oh, I thought, she's not in the mood for this nonsense. Then she surprised me.

"Okay. But no tickling."

"Dang. That was my whole game plan."

TWELVE

FELICIA SEEMED MORE RELAXED when she headed off to work the next morning. Maybe it was the sweet thrill of victory in our little game of chase-and-squeal. Okay, so I let her win, but I thought she needed it, and it's one of those games where everyone goes away a winner.

The only casualty was my shinbone, which bore a huge red scrape from where I'd encountered the coffee table in the dark. Plus, I seemed a little hoarse from squealing.

But enough about that. My first stop of the day was the office of Johnny Land, a real estate speculator I knew. I wouldn't call Johnny a friend. In fact, I can barely stand to be in the same room with him. But I'd done some eviction work for him several years ago and had kept in contact. Never can tell when a ruthless greedhead might come in handy. If anybody knew what Tierra Verde was up to out on the Rio Puerco, it would be Johnny Land.

I knew from our past dealings that Johnny had shortened his name from Landesberg, part of his successful transformation from moneygrubbing shlub to wheeler-dealer. You could see Johnny Land's pug-ugly mug on billboards all over town. He always was painted as being on the go, a cellular phone pressed up against his ear. READY FOR YOUR DREAM HOME? the billboards bellowed. SEE JOHNNY RUN.

The billboards, as loud and obnoxious as Johnny himself, had drawn criticism and, on a couple of occasions, shotgun blasts. But they did the job for Johnny Land. Enough people were stupid enough to choose their real estate agent from big freeway signs that Johnny had become a rich man.

He hadn't gotten so uppity that he'd forgotten me, though. Which was good for him. I was edgy enough that I might've tossed him out the nearest window if he'd tried to stiff me.

The reason for this tension was the location of Johnny's office. Downtown's dominated these days by twin skyscrapers called the Albuquerque Plaza complex. Their pointy roofs had finally given downtown something like a skyline, a personality. But I didn't even like to look at the goddamned things. It was in the smaller of the towers— which held the Hyatt Regency—that I'd first laid eyes on the guy who thought he was Elvis Presley. Ever since that all turned out so badly, I've tried to avoid the place.

But Johnny Land's office was located in the other tower and, if I wanted to see him, I had no choice. I parked underground and rode an elevator to the lobby, with its geometric carpet and its pink marble walls.

I hustled away from the hotel end of the building toward the elevators that serve the office tower. When the bell dinged on the fourteenth floor, I got off, half-expecting somebody to shout, "He-e-r-r-e's Johnny!"

Instead, I found a perfectly normal-looking secretary, who buzzed Johnny right away and sent me to his inner office.

Johnny always looks like an accountant on his way to a costume party, maybe one with a 1970s disco theme. Pale and pudgy, with wire-rimmed glasses and a nose like a Bartlett pear, he wears brightly patterned polyester shirts with wide pointed collars, gold chains around his neck, bell-bottoms. I don't even know where you find clothes like that anymore. Here's Johnny, able to afford the finest tailor-made suits if he wants them, and he's still trying to be John freaking Travolta.

Johnny was rocked back in his chair, his feet up on the desk, showing off patent-leather loafers with tassles on the tops. I hate those. He had a cordless phone to his head, just like on the billboards, and the antenna sticking up made him look like My Favorite Martian on an off day. Johnny had his thin black hair pulled back into a miniature ponytail in the back. Ouch. Another bad fashion decision there, Johnny.

Talking loudly into the phone the whole time, he made finger gestures toward a chair, the wet bar in the corner, one toward the ceiling to indicate he'd be just a minute. I tried not to listen to his bluff, smarmy spiel as I poured myself an expensive bourbon, sniffed it, sat.

Johnny hung up the phone a minute later, leaned across the wide desk to shake my hand.

"Bubba, how ya doin'? Been a long time."

"Sure has, Johnny. You're looking prosperous."

"It's just work, work, work. But people want land, homes, so what can I do?"

I was thinking, You can steal them blind, you little putz you.

"Absolutely," I said. "Things going good, then?"

"Better'n ever. In fact, I got a coupla suits coming in here any minute, gonna try to foist another finder's fee on me."

"You're busy; I'll be brief."

"Take your time. Suits can wait. We're old friends, right?"

Johnny seemed a little desperate for friendship, considering we'd done business only a few times, and that years ago. But I nodded him along and got down to brass tacks.

"Listen, I'm trying to find out about a company up in

Rio Rancho called Tierra Verde. What do you know about it?''

Johnny Land leaked a low whistle, sat back.

"Tierra Verde, huh? You're playing with the big boys now, Bubba."

"That so?"

"Oh yeah. You see the *Gazette* today? They finally announced what most of us already knew. They're going to build a giant planned community up on the West Mesa, other side of the volcanoes. Huge, just huge."

"You got a piece of that?"

"Shit, I wish. But I got plenty to occupy myself without going way over there. People want to live in closer, you know?"

"Right. So what makes Tommy Greene think he can make a go of some big development on the mesa?"

Johnny paused, his mouth open, as if he'd been stricken by a thought.

"You know Tommy Greene?"

I shook my head. "I'd never even heard of him until a couple days ago. You know him?"

Johnny shut his mouth, glanced around the room, like somebody else might be listening. He didn't find anybody, so he continued.

"I wouldn't say I know the man. I met him once, about a year ago, at a restaurant. Somebody I knew introduced us. Spooky dude."

"Yeah? How so?"

"Big guy with blond hair. Bleached, you know? Looks like something off the World Wrestling Federation. You ever watch those clowns? They crack me up."

"Yeah, yeah, but what about Greene?"

"Oh, right. Greene. Nobody knows much about him, but I wouldn't cross him if I were you."

"Why's that?"

"I don't know, he just seemed spooky, you know? Big-city type. Tough guy. Talks out of the side of his mouth."

Johnny tried to demonstrate, but the sight of Johnny Land trying to look tough was too much to bear. I almost burst out laughing in his face.

"So, is it for real, or is it just an act?"

Johnny made a fish face, thinking it over.

"I think it's for real, Bubba. I hear stories, you know—"

"What kind of stories?"

"Chill, man. I was about to tell you. All right?"

"Sorry. Go ahead."

"There's this guy I knew. In the same business as me, but too straight, you know, wouldn't go the billboard route. Name of Bill Silk. You know him?"

I shook my head.

"Well, one day, Smooth-Ass calls me up. That's what we called him, see? From smooth as Silk. Get it?"

I sighed my impatience. Johnny got the message, continued.

"So Smooth-Ass calls me, wants to know what I know about Greene, about Tierra Verde. Hey, just like you, right? So I told him what little I know; then I asked him why he wants to know, and he tells me they're trying to muscle him on some property he's handling over by Rio Rancho."

"'Muscle him'?"

"Yeah, like he told them he wasn't interested in selling and they got tough, you know?"

Just like Harry Whitewoman. This was getting interesting.

"So what happened?"

"So, nothing. I mean, Smooth-Ass tells them to fuck off, figures it's over, right? Then a few days later, he gets a heart attack—the *big one,* you know? I think he's in a nursing home down in Texas now, has to have somebody spoon-feed him Jell-O. Too damned bad.''

Johnny shook his head. When he looked back up at me, there was a glint in his eye.

''But the scuttlebutt was that he didn't have the heart attack all by himself.''

''What do you mean?''

''I mean old Smooth-Ass had some help. Couple of big guys left his office right before his secretary found Smooth-Ass crumpled on the floor like a used Dixie cup. Nobody could prove anything, but the goons were from Tierra Verde, and the assumption in my circle was they were hurting him in some way, or getting in his face, and that caused the old ticker to stop.''

''Jesus.''

''Yeah, bad shit, right? Anyway, since that happened, I've been very careful to avoid Tommy Greene and his dealings. Just makes sense, right?''

''Sure does.''

Johnny checked his watch, looked up at me.

''So, Bubba, I only gotta couple minutes here. What's this all about?''

''I'm not sure. But Tierra Verde keeps coming up in an investigation of mine. Maybe I need to go see Mr. Tommy Greene.''

Johnny clutched at his shirtfront, as if I'd just stopped *his* ticker.

''I wouldn't do that if I were you. Those guys are trouble, you know? I got a nose for this kind of thing.''

I was thinking, You got a nose for draining water beds. But what I said was, ''Don't worry about me, Johnny. I can take care of myself.''

I thanked Johnny Land for his help and showed myself

out, passing two Japanese businessmen jabbering and bowing in the outer office.

Riding down in the elevator, I was wondering, What was David Field doing out there on Tommy Greene's land? Was he working for Greene? And did one of Greene's goons stop Field's heart, too?

THIRTEEN

THE BOURBON HAD GIVEN ME a little buzz. Probably a bad idea to have a drink first thing in the morning, but I hadn't been about to pass up Johnny Land's pricey liquor. Share the wealth, right?

Anyway, the buzz might've emboldened me, I don't know. What I do know is that fifteen minutes later, I was driving up the steep hill that separates Albuquerque from Rio Rancho, on my way to Tierra Verde.

I don't know exactly what I expected. It wasn't as if the suits at the Tierra Verde office were going to take one look at me, fall to their knees, and confess they'd killed David Field. Guess I was just looking for a feeling, a sense of the company, whether it was as scary as everybody said. Sometimes, I just plunge in without thinking and come away with my best information. Other times, I plunge in and come away owing hospital bills. This one looked like it could go either way.

I hardly ever go to Rio Rancho. Nothing there I need, and I always manage to get lost when I do try to find something there. Near as I can tell, Rio Rancho has three straight east-west boulevards. The rest of the town looks like the street engineers tied a paintbrush to a cow's tail and put streets wherever they found paint a week later. Nearly the entire town was built by the same contractor, so the neighborhoods have a remarkable sameness, even more monotonous than the Northeast Heights. That just adds to my confusion. Fortunately, Tierra Verde's address was on Southern Boulevard, one of the straight streets, and I was able to find it and head west.

Since Intel constructed the world's largest computer-chip factory in Rio Rancho, the nature of the town has changed. You're more likely to see nerds with California accents populating its fast-food restaurants. Before Intel, Rio Rancho was like Brooklyn West, peopled by fast-talking retirees looking for the good life in the wide-open spaces. The standing joke about Rio Rancho concerns the number of former gangsters who live here. Word was that the federal Witness Protection Program used Rio Rancho as a snitch relocation point. Mobster rats out his buddies, and the federal government buys him a nice cracker box near the golf course in Rio Rancho. He lives happily ever after, hacking bogies and bitching about how you can't get a decent bagel out west.

Of course, that gave the town a palpable uneasiness. You don't want to think the nice old man who lives down the street might've been a hit man in his former life. You don't want to become pals with a neighbor, only to find out his middle name is "the."

Lot of local people moved to Rio Rancho, too. They might give up a certain charm, their lawns might be loose, blowing sand, and they might spend an hour each day commuting back and forth into Albuquerque, but at least they could afford the mortgage and other little necessities, like food. Life among retired gangsters might not be so bad, if it's all you can afford.

The Tierra Verde office sat in the middle of a hedge-trimmed parking lot near the western edge of Rio Rancho. The building squatted wide and low, covered in brown stucco and white trim—what's known out here as Territorial Style. I parked near the front door and spent a full two minutes deciding whether to hook the Smith & Wesson into my belt. Finally, I opted to leave it in the glove compartment. I'm just a private eye visiting a public place of business. What could happen?

I checked my hair in the rearview mirror, tucked at my shirttail, got out of the truck, and strode through the company's door as if I belonged there.

A receptionist filed her red talons at a wide desk that blocked further encroachment. She was middle-aged, wore the secretary's requisite seven pounds of makeup and an expression like she'd just chewed a lemon.

"Hi there," I said brightly. "I'd like to speak to Tommy Greene."

She gave me a baleful stare. I wondered what kind of Rio Rancho resident she was—East Coast, West Coast, local. She opened her mouth and confirmed my first impression—flat, nasal, Brooklyn.

"You got an appointment?"

"No. My name is Bubba Mabry. I'm a private investigator." I flashed her my ID.

"And what would be your business with Mr. Greene?"

"I'm investigating the death of a man who was killed out by the Rio Puerco. His body was found on land owned by Tierra Verde."

If this shook her, it didn't show.

"Sorry. Mr. Greene sees no one without an appointment."

"I really must insist. This is a murder investigation, you understand. Real important."

"Look, sugar, I don't care if the Pope himself comes waltzing through that door wanting to confirm sainthood on Mr. Greene. If he's got no appointment, he's outta here."

"I don't think you understand—"

She reached across the desk, pushed a button that sounded a buzzer somewhere behind her. Then she crossed her arms, looked up at me, and almost smiled. That worried me.

A door behind her swung open and was filled by a weight lifter disguised as a Jaycee. He wore his black hair buzzed flat on top, so it just cleared the top of the doorway. He was dressed in a green polo shirt pulled tightly across his pecs, yuppie loafers on big wide feet, and a gray suit that looked as if it had been specially made to accommodate the bulging muscles that stood out from his shoulders in all directions. He had a heavy brow that shaded his eyes, and a jaw like a shovel. Frankenstein meets the Incredible Hulk.

"You rang?" he said, just like that giant butler on TV. What was his name? Lurch.

"This gentleman," the secretary brayed, "insists on seeing Mr. Greene. He's got no appointment."

Lurch strode across the room and stood very close to me. I felt as if I could hide in his shadow. Up close, I could see his deep tan came from a tanning booth rather than from outdoor living. He had no lines at the corner of his eyes, none of the wear and tear the Southwest sun produces.

"My name's Bob Barron. Can I help you?"

Programmed to say that. What he means is, Which wall should I pitch you through?

I quickly explained who I was and what I wanted.

"No appointment?"

"Well, no, but—"

"Then I'll have to ask you to leave."

"This doesn't seem like a very friendly way to do business."

Bob flexed his shoulders, twisted his thick neck back and

forth, as if he wasn't accustomed to arguments and they gave him a pain.

"You're not here for business," he said. "You're being a pest. You got no appointment. I don't hafta be friendly."

As if the tons of muscles weren't convincing enough, Barron casually stuck his thick hand into his pants pocket, in the process pulling back his suit coat so I could see the big revolver hanging on a swing rig under his arm. Shit.

My feet practically turned around backward on my ankles as they tried to take me to the door, but my mouth wasn't finished yet.

"How about this? How about I talk to Mr. Flick?"

Flick the Flack. Guess that name stuck in my mind when Felicia told me about it. It popped into my head and out my mouth just in the nick of time.

"You know Sammy?" the side of beef asked.

"Oh, yeah. Me and Sammy go way back."

Barron looked like he didn't believe me, but he finally said, "I'll go get him."

He turned and disappeared through the door, into the bowels of the building. The secretary had gone back to filing her nails, uninterested in the drama unfolding between bouncer and bungler. Guess she'd seen it too many times before.

My shirt was soaked with flop sweat. My feet danced, ready to run. I sorely missed my trusty pistol, locked up safe and sound outside in my truck. What a putz I am. Everybody warned me Tierra Verde hired goons. I come face-to-face with the gooniest of them all, and my gun's nowhere handy. Great planning.

Bob Barron reappeared in the doorway, filling it with his wide shoulders, and it wasn't until he stepped aside that I could see the little eel squirming into the room behind him.

Sammy Flick looked like a soldier in the Army of Nervous Smiles, Flinch Division—as if he'd spent a lifetime ducking bigger guys, laughing at their jokes, heh-heh, and telling them how important they were. He weighed maybe a hundred pounds, he was losing his hair, and his high forehead seemed glazed with sweat. The sweat played hell with his thick eyeglasses, which he repeatedly pushed up a slippery nose that looked like a thumb.

Sammy adjusted his glasses and stared at me a second.

"I've never seen this guy before in my life."

Uh-oh. Barron bunched his eyebrows. The man even had overdeveloped muscles in his face.

"Ah, Mr. Flick, yes, well, we haven't actually met before—"

"You said you was old friends." Barron wasn't going to let this slip by him. He'd seized on my little deception like a snapping turtle.

"Well, that's not exactly what I meant. I know Sammy's *reputation* as an honest spokesman. That's really what I meant when I said we went way back. I mean I know *of* him—"

Sammy Flick cut me off.

"What is that you want, mister?"

I told him I was a private investigator, that I was looking into David Field's murder. He glanced Barron's way, and it seemed that some slight communication flickered between them. Then Flick quickly covered it up by saying, "Follow me to my office."

I did, practically skipping past Bob the Brute. I'd won this round, but I wouldn't want to go many others with someone of Barron's physical superiority and mental limitations.

Flick led me down a hall and around a corner, then into a small office. As we walked, I glanced through the open doors of other offices. Two or three were filled with fast-talking salesmen types, feet up on their desks, phones to their heads. In a corridor, I saw a red-haired guy of the approximate physical dimensions of Bob Barron just sitting and reading a newspaper. What does a land-development company need with guys like that? Just to push around old Indians?

Sammy sat behind his desk, twitched, pushed up his glasses. His hair looked wet from the constant sheen on his head. This is the guy a company chooses for its front man?

"So, Mr. Mabry, what do you want me to say? We know about Mr. Field's death, of course, and we're as puzzled as anyone else."

"He wasn't working for you?"

Flick looked surprised by that question. "No. Never."

"Then what was he doing on Tierra Verde land?"

"A very good question. Trespassing, I think, is the only answer. We hadn't authorized it."

"Might somebody have shot him for trespassing?"

Flick tried pushing up the other side of his glasses, but they slid right down again.

"Hardly. We didn't even know he was there until the sheriff's department contacted us. There's a lot of empty land out there, Mr. Mabry. We can hardly be held responsible every time someone wants to sneak onto it."

We were getting nowhere fast.

"I was looking at a map," I said. "And it looked to me that the place where David Field was killed is right in the middle of where you're putting your new development."

Flick blinked rapidly.

"We wouldn't want that getting around. This is a very important time for the company. Some people might not like to live at a murder scene. It might taint the development. Mr. Greene wouldn't like that."

Sammy Flick had the hunted look of a guy whose job

depends on keeping somebody happy. Mr. Greene, from everything I'd heard, didn't sound like a naturally happy man.

"What about me talking to Mr. Greene?"

"Mr. Greene is a very private person."

"So I've heard. But I'd only need a few minutes of his time."

"I'm afraid that wouldn't be possible. Mr. Greene sees no one without an appointment."

"How do I get an appointment?"

"Mr. Greene makes all his own appointments."

"So, he'd have to call me, huh?"

"Something like that. You can leave your card with the receptionist—"

"But I'd be wasting my time."

Flick winced, shrugged. He glanced over at something on his desk, and I followed the glance and saw a button like the one the receptionist had pushed to summon Bob Barron. No chance of getting tough with Sammy Flick. Not unless I wanted to duke it out with Hulkenstein.

I bid Sammy Flick the fondest of farewells and got the hell out of there.

FOURTEEN

I WAS ON MY WAY DOWN the big hill toward Albuquerque when I spotted the tail. I don't know what possessed me to check the mirrors. It wasn't as if Sammy Flick or Bob Barron had any reason to follow me. Clearly, I knew nothing that posed any threat to them. I knew nothing, period.

I guess I was rewinding the mental tape on my encounter with Tierra Verde, and something about that got me looking in the mirrors, and there it was—a black Chevy Cavalier, the kind of small, anonymous auto you see on rental-car lots. It followed me down the hill to the giant intersection at Coors and Alameda. The car had been keeping its distance, but it had to come up right behind me at the intersection, close enough for me to see that the guy behind the wheel had swimmer's shoulders and a porkpie hat like Gene Hackman wore in *The French Connection*. Maybe that's what got me noticing. People don't wear hats like that here. They either go for the cowboy look or they wear baseball caps like everywhere else in the Western world. The hat brim shaded the guy's face, so I couldn't make it out, but from the movements of his head, he seemed to be going to a lot of trouble to look uninterested in my big red truck. He turned south onto Coors, following right behind me.

Coors Road is a good place to die. It's a broad four-lane that skirts the flank of the mesa all the way from the shady village of Corrales in the north to the rural South Valley. People drive it as fast as a freeway, but Coors has red lights and trucks turning and an outstanding view of the Sandias and the whole city spread out in the bowl below. You get to looking over there, admiring the vista, and pretty soon you're zooming up to a red light at sixty miles an hour and it's screech, scream, boom.

I always make a point of watching carefully and hugging the shoulder in the slow lane when I drive on Coors, trying not to become another one of its statistics. But now there was this black Cavalier dawdling back there behind me, and I could barely watch the road for watching the mirrors.

I didn't know what Porkpie wanted, but I sure didn't want him following me home. Very few people knew I lived at Felicia's now, and I tried to keep it that way. The phone book still gave my old number, but Information would refer callers to Felicia's number. I still got my mail at a post office box near the Cruise, not that I received much. All the bills, magazines, and junk mail at home came addressed to Felicia Quattlebaum.

Time for some fancy driving. I didn't know the guy in the Cavalier, but if he was part of Tierra Verde, that probably meant he was from back east somewhere and that he wouldn't know Albuquerque like I do. This was my town, and I'd be damned if some Yankee could outmaneuver me on its back streets. I followed the cloverleaf curl onto eastbound Interstate 40 and gave the Ram its head, zooming toward downtown.

The Ram's got all the acceleration you're going to get out of a vehicle that big, and I managed to put some distance between me and the tail. But he wouldn't have any trouble finding me again. The truck's anything but inconspicuous. When it was left to me by the late publisher of the *Albuquerque Gazette,* I entertained thoughts of trading it for something as anonymous as the faded old Chevy Nova I drove before. You can't do stakeout work in something that looks like a fire truck. But months had passed, and I was still driving the big old eye-grabber. Truth is, Albuquerque's so populated with pickup trucks that the Ram wouldn't get much attention if it weren't so damned *red*.

As I roared across the river, I could see the Cavalier closing. The freeway teemed with late-afternoon traffic, and he probably couldn't get as close as he might like. I planned to take advantage of that.

Catching the traffic lights right was the trick to this. I veered down an exit ramp at the last second, roared downhill to Twelfth Street, hit the light going yellow—yes!—and blew on through. I went up the frontage road, barely catching a green at Sixth, then back up on the freeway via a steep ramp at Fourth. Picking up speed, I whistled past the graveyard where the two interstates intersect, then took I-25 going south toward downtown. The Cavalier was nowhere to be seen. I couldn't stop grinning, practically blinded myself with it in my mirrors.

I got off the crowded freeway at what used to be the Grand Avenue exit, which now sports extra-long signs to hold its new name: Dr. Martin Luther King Jr. Avenue. Just a few more blocks to Central, and then east toward the Cruise.

I felt like celebrating, like wandering into one of the beer joints I used to haunt and telling my buddies how smooth I'd been escaping the tail. But a glance at my watch told me I'd better get to Felicia's. She'd be home soon, and she'd probably have dinner plans and more wedding tactics to discuss. I wasn't even married yet, and I already acted like somebody's husband.

It took another twenty minutes to get there, rolling along

the Cruise, then north on surface streets. I turned into the parking lot and let the Ram idle along as I looked for a place to park it. I kept my eyes open for a black Cavalier, in case the sumbitch had pulled an end run on me.

No sign of him, but it was a good thing I was looking. In a corner of the parking lot, in an emerald green Ford, sat a guy reading a newspaper. You know, that might work in New York or somewhere. Guy reading a newspaper, waiting for somebody at the curb, you think nothing of it. But nobody does that in Albuquerque. Especially in the parking lot of an apartment complex. Especially when it's ninety degrees outside.

I swung the Ram into a space where I could watch the Ford in the mirror, paused with my hand on the door handle. The newspaper drooped and Bob Barron glared over the top of it at me. No mistaking that square head and those close-knit brows.

It took the wind out of my sails, I must confess. I thought I'd been so smooth shaking Porkpie, but maybe he'd let me escape. All the while, Bob Barron was tracking down my address and coming here to wait for me. Tierra Verde must have quite an information network for him to find me so quickly. Course, he could've called Information, got my new number, done a quick look through a crisscross directory, found where Felicia lived...aw, hell.

I couldn't just sit there in the truck, cursing myself, without Bob the Beast figuring out that I'd spotted him. I got out of the truck and sauntered toward the apartment, making a point of not glancing his way. As soon as I rounded a corner, I tore up the stairs, let myself into the apartment, and dashed across the living room to peak out the window. Still there, though he wasn't pretending to read the paper anymore.

"What are you doing?"

Felicia's voice startled me so, I nearly jumped out the window. I clutched my chest, whirled around, looking for my composure.

"I, uh…oh, hi, hon, I didn't know you were home."

She gave me a look like one of those neckless owls out in the desert.

"Got off early. What are you doing at the window?"

"Well, see, I think I'm being followed. Guy down there. No big deal."

Felicia stepped to the window, pulled back the curtain.

I snatched it away from her and closed it. I didn't want Bob to know we were watching him back.

"What's the matter with you?"

She yanked the curtain out of my hand and practically pressed her nose against the glass. A perfect target.

"The guy in the green car?"

"Yeah. You want to come away from there?"

"Who is he?"

"Come away from the window and I'll tell you all about it."

She gave me a frown, but she moved back. I sighed. Now I'd have to keep up my end of the hurriedly made bargain. Damn. I really didn't want Felicia involved in all this—whatever it was—and I didn't want her to know what a bust I'd been at the Tierra Verde office. If they knew to follow me here, then they knew I was shacked up with the pushy reporter who'd been snooping into their affairs. The overall equation added up to trouble.

But I'd rather take on a whole roomful of goons like Bob Barron than tangle with Felicia. I quickly told her about my visit to Tierra Verde, Sammy Flick, Bob Barron.

"The guy in the car is Barron. I guess they sent him to keep an eye on me."

I couldn't imagine Barron having the initiative to find

me on his own. My guess was Sammy Flick tracked me down, then sent Barron here.

"Bastards!"

"Easy now, Felicia. There's nothing we can do about it without stirring up a lot of problems. If we just ignore him, he'll go away eventually."

"I'm not going to ignore him!"

She turned and marched toward the door.

"Wait!" I grabbed the sleeve of her Hawaiian shirt, but she turned and gave my hand such a withering look, the skin practically melted off the bones. I let go and followed her downstairs, whining about how she shouldn't bother the surveillance.

Barron saw her coming across the parking lot, tried to hide behind his newspaper, saw it was no good. His window was rolled down, and Felicia stuck her head right in there, getting within inches of his thick, stricken face.

"What the hell are you doing?"

Barron's lips went tight. He clearly wasn't accustomed to people challenging him. But he didn't seem to have the mental reserves to retort.

"Tommy Greene sent you, didn't he?"

Barron managed to shake his head, though it came off like the slightest of swivels on his giant neck.

"I don't know what you're talking about. I'm waiting on someone."

"Yeah? Who?"

"None of your business."

I hung back ten feet or so, wringing my hands, thinking, Don't get him angry, baby. If he gets out of that car, I'm going to have to try to stop him from hurting you, and he'll snap me like a dry twig. I thought of my pistol, measured the space between where I stood and the Ram, decided it was hopeless. Some storms you just ride out.

"I don't need this cloak-and-dagger shit in my parking lot." Felicia's voice rose to a howl. "I've got a wedding to plan!"

Barron blinked, trying to process information that was beyond him.

"Now get out of this parking lot before I call the cops!"

He took a deep breath and turned his head so he was staring straight ahead, but he made no move to start the car.

"Yeah?" he said. "What are you going to tell the cops?"

"That you're trespassing, for one. That I think you're stalking me. That you're some kind of pervert who gets off on watching women's windows. You think they won't be here in minutes?"

A flush spread up Barron's wide face. Even he could see this was going badly. He reached for the keys.

"And you tell Tommy Greene this for me," she shouted. "If he wants to harass me, he ought to be man enough to face me himself, instead of sending his errand boy."

Barron clenched his muscular teeth. The car's engine roared to life, and Felicia pulled her head out of the window just in time. I had to dance out of the way as the car zoomed toward the parking lot's exit.

I turned, to find Felicia smiling.

"I think you made him mad."

"Wasn't it great? Maybe now Tommy Greene will have to come out of his hidey-hole."

"I'm not sure that was a good idea."

She frowned at me.

"Bubba, you can't let guys like that push you around. You can outsmart them."

I couldn't remember the last time I'd outsmarted anybody. I thought I'd accomplished something evading the

Cavalier, only to find they'd beaten me to the punch. And now my fiancée could take all the credit for standing up to Bob Barron.

Dang.

FIFTEEN

TUESDAY MORNING, THE PHONE woke me. I looked at the alarm clock and the empty space in the bed beside me. Nearly nine o'clock. Felicia already at work, and me piled up in bed like a hibernating grizzly. I rolled over, found the phone on the sixth ring, answered. "Hullo?"

"Mr. Mabry? Anna Lipscomb calling."

It took me a second, since I was drunk with sleep, but I recognized the name from the Biology Department. The thought of the chairwoman's stern schoolmarm face made me sit up in bed.

"Yes, ma'am. What can I do for you?"

"I'd like to talk with you—in person. Can you stop by my office?"

I had no plan for the day. Tierra Verde had exhausted my possibilities, and I'd gotten nowhere there. Even though I'd given the case considerable thought the night before while Felicia prattled on about the wedding reception, I didn't know where to turn next. The thought of wasting more time with Anna Lipscomb didn't appeal, but it was better than nothing.

"Sure. What time?"

"How about in an hour? I'm on my way to a class, but I'll be finished by then."

Let's see. I needed coffee, a newspaper, a shower, a shave, clean clothes.

"That'll be fine."

She hung up without saying good-bye, which I took as a bad sign. I resisted the temptation to fall back onto my pillow. Instead, I got up and got busy.

I was only a couple of minutes late for my appointment. I would've been on time if I hadn't had so much trouble finding a parking spot for the Ram. I ended up parking illegally three blocks away, in the parking lot of a church. The church sits right behind a convenience store that's popular with junkies and street people. The church has a needle-thin steeple, so naturally everybody calls it Our Lady of the Hypodermic.

I hoofed it into the Biology Department, down the hall to the department office, and right up to Monica Gallegos's desk. She'd gone robin's egg blue in her wardrobe choice today and she wore matching eye shadow and maroon lipstick. How can someone spend that much time on their appearance and get anything accomplished in life? I'm lucky if I remember to run a comb through my thinning hair once a day.

Monica was expecting me. She gave me a cross look, perhaps not forgiving me (or herself) for the blubbering scene the first time we met. She seemed to be holding up better now that she'd had a chance to adjust to the idea of David Field being dead.

"Ms. Lipscomb is expecting you," she said flatly. "Go right in."

So I did, thinking, though, that I needed to talk to Monica Gallegos about Field. If universities work like most companies, the secretaries are the ones who really run the show. After my experiences with Anna Lipscomb and the strange Emil Pugh, fragrant Monica Gallegos seemed like the most normal one in the building.

Anna Lipscomb wore black today, loose and shapeless

cotton like before. Her hair was pulled back so tightly that I wondered whether she had a lot of facial wrinkles she was trying to smooth out. She didn't stand when I entered, just pointed me into the same threadbare orange chair as before.

"Mr. Mabry, thanks for coming. This should only take a few minutes, but I thought it better if it came face-to-face rather than over the phone."

Sounded like bad news, and I didn't need any more of that. Anna Lipscomb took a deep breath, as if she needed extra air to spew whatever was to come.

"I understand you went yesterday to see a man named Tommy Greene?"

"Word travels fast."

"Yes, well, Mr. Greene seems to have many influential friends, including at least one on the board of regents."

"Regents?"

"They run the school, Mr. Mabry. They're the ones who approve departmental budgets and hire faculty and decide who gets a new building around here."

"Okay. So you got a phone call."

"Yes, I did. And the person who called was very troubled by the way you're snooping around in David Field's death."

"Is that so? I'd be interested in knowing who that might be."

Her lips did that disappearing act. No wonder Anna Lipscomb didn't wear lipstick. As many times a day as those lips went into her mouth, she'd overdose on the stuff.

"I'm sure you would like to know," she said. "And you can understand why I won't tell you."

I waited her out a while, but it wasn't going anywhere, so finally I nodded.

"You have to understand, Mr. Mabry, I have to look to

the future. I'm as sorry as anyone that David Field is dead, but I can't sit by while you cause problems for my department.''

''And *you* have to understand that I conduct my investigations any way I please. Whether your department gets new toys from the board of regents doesn't interest me. I've got a job to do.''

Bing-bang with the lips. A grudging nod.

''I know I can't stop you,'' she said. ''I just thought I should tell you that you're causing problems for us—and probably for no good reason. It sounds to be as if Tommy Greene and his company couldn't possibly have anything to do with David's murder.''

I shrugged.

''Maybe that's true. I don't know yet. They sure are balky about talking about him, though.''

''I'm not surprised. My understanding is they're embarking on an expensive, risky development plan. They don't need bad publicity. No wonder Mr. Greene's pulling strings.''

''Yeah, but if he's got nothing to hide, why bother calling up some regent and getting that person to lean on you?''

Anna Lipscomb stood, her fingertips resting on her desk. My time was running out.

''And,'' I added quickly, ''it looks like David Field was on Greene's land when he got offed.''

She winced at my choice of words, shook her head slowly.

''David wasn't authorized to be out there, not by Tierra Verde and not by this department. Simply put, he was trespassing. The fact that someone found him out there and killed him doesn't change that.''

''No, but the fact he was trespassing doesn't make him any less dead.''

She frowned, gave me the stiff back.

"You're not a very pleasant person, are you, Mr. Mabry?"

"I think I'm insulted."

"Don't mock me. You're gruff and rude and headstrong, and you enjoy making trouble for other people, don't you?"

"I don't know what you mean. I think of myself as a southern gentleman."

She didn't smile, probably hadn't in years.

"I think you're probably in over your head this time. You don't know it yet, but you're fooling with the wrong people."

"You mean Greene?"

"I mean myself, for one," she said icily. "And others, behind the scenes. You might be better off if you found yourself another investigation to pursue."

She watched me down her long nose, waiting for my response. I crossed my legs, leaned back in the rickety chair.

"You know, if I quit every time somebody got their feathers ruffled, I'd never finish an investigation."

"I assure you, Mr. Mabry, we're talking about more than feathers here. We're talking land, money, and the future of Albuquerque."

"Is that so?"

She watched me, saying nothing for a long minute.

"Good day, Mr. Mabry."

A southern gentleman knows when he's being shown the door. I let myself out, leaving Anna Lipscomb standing imperiously at her desk. I was careful not to slam the door.

Monica Gallegos was missing from her desk in the outer office. I was starting to get the feeling she was avoiding me. I thought about prowling the building, finding other colleagues of Field's to interview, but Anna Lipscomb probably had put the word out about me. Besides, I was hungry. Time for a breakfast burrito at Garcia's and some rumination about where the case was going—or, more accurately, why it was going nowhere.

I exited the building and was walking past the cactus garden when Monica Gallegos stepped out from behind a concrete pillar and called my name.

Guess she wasn't avoiding me after all. Just lying in wait out of Lipscomb's sight. I strolled over to her, checking out her hands (empty) and her blue suit (pleasantly full).

"Hi there. I've been wanting to talk to you."

She glanced over her shoulder and past mine, making sure no one was watching.

"Yeah, well, I've got a few things to say to you, but it's gotta be quick."

She had a trace of a Spanish lilt when she talked fast, and the words spilled rapidly now.

"You've probably found out by now that I had a romance with David Field. I wanted to tell you I had nothing to do with his death."

I tried not to fall off my shoes.

"Um, right. That's why I wanted to speak to you."

She nodded, as if I'd confirmed her suspicions.

"People talk, I know that. I should've known better than to get involved with David, but I made a mistake. David could be very persuasive. And he walked all over anybody who got in his way."

The words were out before I'd considered how they'd sound: "And he cheated on his wife."

She flushed under the Estée Lauder, nodded quickly.

"Yes, he did. And not just with me. There were others when he was seeing me, and there were others before."

"And you think one of these paramours killed him?"

She sighed deeply, shrugged a padded shoulder.

"I don't know. I didn't do it, but one of the others might've. David was a hard man to let go of."

"Your relationship with him—it was a long time ago?"

She glanced away.

"Yeah. I thought I was over him completely, until I found out he was dead. Then I fell all to pieces. You saw me here the other day, how I was. The man had a way about him, a way of getting under your skin."

"What about Amber Field? She didn't know about you, about the others?"

"I think she knew. I think she's known all along how he was and she just chose to put the best face on it."

I thought about Amber's reaction when I'd mentioned the gossip about her husband. If she was in denial, it was hip-deep and rising. How long had she been refusing to believe the rumors?

Monica Gallegos glanced around again. Classes must've let out or something, because the pedestrian count suddenly had risen.

"I should go," she said. "I just wanted to set the record straight about me and David. You believe me, don't you?"

"Sure." What wasn't to believe? Monica Gallegos's confession confirmed everything I'd heard about David Field, and then some.

I thanked her, and she hurried into the building without a backward glance. I watched other people entering and leaving the building. I wondered which of the coeds had slept with David Field.

How had Field gotten away with it? I wasn't even married to Felicia yet, but I'd been faithful to her since we first started dating. Not that I hadn't been tempted, but I feared Felicia, plain and simple, and I didn't want to find out how she'd react to infidelity. Field, on the other hand, apparently brimmed with audacity, throwing his big tanned body around while his wife sat at home, denying the truth. Or plotting his murder.

SIXTEEN

IT WAS LATE AFTERNOON before I got home. I'd chased a few leads at the university, including the public affairs office's file of news releases on Field, but I turned up nothing that would tip me to who killed him. He'd been quite a celebrated researcher and a popular teacher (especially with the females), but he'd stayed away from campus controversies and social functions. A lone wolf, this David Field, too busy making discoveries and porking women other than his wife to join in university life.

I was weary when I got to Felicia's apartment complex, and maybe that's why I didn't do a better job of checking the parking lot for someone lying in wait. I slammed the truck door and trudged toward the apartment, lost in my thoughts.

Then a loud crack split the air, and something pinged off the asphalt at my feet.

"Holy shi—"

Crack! Something buzzed past my head like an angry hummingbird.

I took two quick steps and flung myself forward, over a sidewalk and onto the strip of irrigated grass that encircles the apartment building like a green moat. I hit, rolled, and scrambled on all fours into the evergreen shrubs that grow against the building. Not much room under there, but I squirmed on my belly, becoming at one with the dank earth.

The gun popped again, but I couldn't tell how close the bullet came. Then tires squealed in the parking lot, and I got just a glimpse of a small white car roaring away.

I pushed myself out from under the bushes and cautiously got to my feet. No more shots. I ran for the Ram, climbed behind the wheel, and cranked up the engine. Then I zoomed out into the side street, swung into the rush-hour traffic without slowing, and drove half a mile without finding anybody suspicious in a little white car. The shooter had disappeared.

I finally gave up my search after driving up and down Wyoming for a while. My hands were trembling, my throat was dry, and my clothes were covered with mud and burrs from the shrubs.

I'd cured everything but the shakes by the time Felicia got home an hour later. Clean clothes helped; so did bourbon. My throat was well lubricated, but old Jim Beam couldn't touch my trembling.

Felicia looked steamed when she burst through the door. Her face was flushed and a strand of brown hair clung to the dampness across her forehead. A cigarette dangled from her lip, and she puffed smoke as she threw her keys and heavy purse on an end table. It was like a freight train had just rumbled into the room.

She paused when she saw the whiskey bottle, then gave me the hard eye.

"Little early for cocktails, isn't it?"

I'd thought about not mentioning the shots to her. She wouldn't respond well to the thought of somebody trying to bump off her bridegroom. Think how my death would mess up the wedding.

"Rough day," I said, taking another swallow of the warm booze.

"Me, too. Spent the whole day fighting with Sammy Flick, that little jerk up at Tierra Verde."

"He's giving you a hard time, huh?" This was good. So far, she was too caught up in her own day to notice my hands shaking like dogs shedding water.

She came around behind me, talked closer to my ear.

"I'm not saying he's a dickhead, but I'll bet he needs a rabbi to help him get his hat off."

I smiled. That was so like Felicia. My shrinking violet, my fragile flower.

"I accused him of sending that guy—what's his name, Barron?—to spy on us, but he just denied it. Said he didn't know anybody that fit that description."

"I saw the guy at Tierra Verde!"

"I know you did. I told him that, too, but he said you must've been mistaken."

"Damn it, now *I'm* getting mad at the little weasel. I know what I saw."

She kneaded my shoulders.

"I know you did, Bubba. The guy's a professional liar. He's gotta deny it."

I nodded, took another sip. The brown liquid jiggled in the glass as I raised it to my lips.

"Whatsamatter with you?"

Damn, I should've known she'd notice.

"Just a little palsy. Advanced age, you know."

I'm a few years older than Felicia, and I never miss a chance to remind her of it.

"Maybe you ought to see a doctor. Shaking's not good."

She came around the table, looked closely into my eyes. She seemed genuinely worried, which made me feel like a heel for not telling her right away that someone had tried to plug me in the parking lot.

I came clean. Felicia's eyes widened as I told her the story.

"You're sure they were shooting at you?"

"Well, if they weren't, they could've fooled me. One of the shots whizzed right past my head."

"Jesus, Bubba, did you call the cops?"

"No, I—"

"No? You call them right now."

She crossed to the end table where the phone sat, snatched it up to give it to mc.

"No, no. I don't want the cops involved. The sheriff's department is already pissed at me for investigating the Field murder."

"But we can't let the bastards take potshots at you and just get away with it!"

"I'd rather handle it my own way."

"And that would be how? Sitting here shaking and getting drunk?"

"Seems like a good start."

"I think you should at least file a report."

"And tell them what? I didn't get a look at the shooter, barely saw the car."

"I'll bet it was that guy who was watching us yesterday. He knows where we live."

"I thought about that, but it was a different car. And I get the feeling Bob Barron wouldn't miss me with three tries."

"Then who?"

I shook my head. The booze was making me dizzy.

"I don't know. I suppose it could be somebody else from Tierra Verde"—the black Cavalier flashed through my mind—"but I don't know how we'd prove it."

Felicia paced a circle around the table.

"Maybe we could find one of the bullets!"

"Not worth it. One went off the asphalt, so it's mangled somewhere. The others went high. They might've traveled five hundred yards before they hit something."

"But if we could find one, the police might be able to match it up."

"Match it with what? The ones they pull out of me when the shooter gets a better crack at me next time?"

Felicia patted me on the shoulder as she circled past.

"Now, don't get dramatic. I was thinking they might be able to match it with the bullets they took from David Field's body."

I shrugged off her hand.

"I don't want to go out there right now, poking around, maybe digging a bullet out of a wall. I'd rather not give them another chance to pop caps at me, okay?"

She sighed, gave me another pat, slumped onto the sofa.

"How about some food? We could order in pizza, let 'em shoot at the delivery boy."

"I'm not hungry."

"Tough. You need to eat something if you're going to pour down that bourbon. I'm in no mood to hold your head while you barf into the toilet."

True love conquers all.

I told her to order the pizza, but my thoughts were elsewhere. Maybe I *should* go look for those bullets. I'm no expert on guns, but the flat crack of the pistol that shot at me was almost certainly a .22, the same caliber that killed David Field.

SEVENTEEN

FUNERALS GIVE ME THE HEEBIES. I don't like seeing stiffs in their preserved state any more than I do finding them in the desert. Not to mention all the pomp and the flowers, the wailing and the sermonizing, *and* you're supposed to wear a necktie. Felicia has explained to me about catharsis and closure and all that, but I still don't get it. You go to one of these rituals to say good-bye to the one person who can't hear it.

I was jumpy as a frog on ice, but I wasn't going to miss David Field's funeral. I figured the church would be wall-to-wall with suspects, particularly shapely women who might've planted bullets in Field's cultivated brain. I slipped on my trusty blue blazer, buttoned my shirt to the collar (hinting at a tie, or perhaps pretending it had fallen off on my way to the funeral), and stopped by a florist to pin a carnation to my lapel, hiding a coffee strain there. I drove to French Mortuary in the Ram, parked near the back, and cautiously circled the building to enter the chapel. Nobody shot at me.

I didn't drop my guard once inside, despite all the atmospherics aimed at keeping me calm: limp organ music and subdued lighting, thick carpets and restrained sniffling. God, I hated these things. Felicia had promised me she'd be there to keep me from running, shrieking, out of the chapel. She was covering the funeral for the *Gazette* anyway, and she promised it wouldn't distract her too much to have me sweating and twitching next to her.

I walked down the center aisle, whipping my head around in search of her. I must've looked like Loony Lonnie, this old man in a grungy trench coat who's always marching up and down the Cruise. Lonnie thinks he's being followed, so every second or third step, he's compelled to whirl completely around to see who's behind him. It can startle the hell out of you.

I twitched and spun down the aisle, and I finally spotted Felicia sitting at the far end of a pew, about four rows back from the roped-off spot where the dreaded David lay in a (thankfully) closed box. I waved and made my way toward her, veering around a handful of women who'd clustered in the aisle, touching hankies to their eyes and talking in low voices about their grief. I wondered which of them had slept with David Field. Maybe they were comparing notes on the loss to American bedrooms. Death of a Swordsman.

Just as I turned into Felicia's pew, a hand grasped my arm, turned me around. I found myself standing much too close to Etta Dangler. I felt the heat off her breasts, only an inch from my chest, felt the animal pull of her.

"Hi there, Bubba boy."

You wouldn't think a plain black dress could do so much for a woman. Or maybe it was what the woman did for the dress. Either way, it was hard to look at Etta Dangler without going weak-kneed. The dress looked painted onto her voluptuous body. The red hair was like a bonfire. She watched me through lowered eyelids, assessing my reaction to her careful preparations. Apparently, I ogled enough to satisfy her, because she flashed a smile like a lightning bolt.

"I thought I'd see you here," she said.

"Yeah. Pay my respects, you know. Part of the job."

How come I became tongue-tied every time I laid eyes

on this woman? Maybe my tongue had a mind of its own and it was busy thinking about regions of Etta Dangler it would like to explore.

"How's your investigation going? You finding lots of clues?"

"It's going all right."

Etta Dangler cut her eyes around the room.

"Probably plenty of suspects right here, huh, sugar?"

I looked around, too, as if she might be communicating something to me, but all I saw were formless mourners. I couldn't seem to focus on anyone but the woman right in front of me.

Then I got a tap on the shoulder.

"Huh? Oh, hi, Felicia. Felicia! Hi!"

Felicia glared at me. She wore a straight black dress with a little jacket over it, the outfit I'd seen her put on three hours earlier. She called it her "funeral suit." I guess every reporter has one. She looked nice, despite her big glasses and her wind-strung hair and the overall sense of familiarity we shared. But I didn't get a chance to tell her because I was too busy not quite apologizing for the attention I'd paid Etta Dangler.

"Felicia, I'd like you to meet Etta Dangler. She's a friend of Amber Field's. She's been talking to me about my case. She's interested in who killed Field, too. Ms. Dangler, this is my fiancée, Felicia Quattlebaum."

The subtext here: I never touched her, Felicia. I'm not attracted to this bombshell. It's all business.

Felicia looked through me. Jealousy, competitiveness, and general claw baring charged the air between her and Etta Dangler. I wanted very badly to be elsewhere.

"Guess we ought to sit. Looks like they'll start soon."

Felicia watched Etta. "Wouldn't you like to join us, Ms. Dangler?"

Etta demurred, saying she was sitting with friends on the far side of the chapel. I whewed in relief. She purred her good-byes, and I followed Felicia back to where she'd been sitting.

Felicia didn't look at me right away. I felt shamefaced and edgy, even though I hadn't done anything wrong. Okay, maybe I had some thoughts that I shouldn't have, being an almost-married man and all, but Felicia wasn't supposed to be privy to those. It's one of my great failings that people, in particular Felicia, can read my face like it's a freaking billboard.

"So," Felicia muttered, "that one of your suspects?"

"Ahem. Maybe. She claims she's about the only woman in town who *wasn't* sleeping with David Field."

Felicia snorted.

"I can't imagine that woman practicing such self-restraint."

That woman—Felicia had sized up Etta Dangler, and her verdict wasn't pretty. I tried an appeal to her newshound instincts.

"Lots of the other players are here, too."

I turned around in the pew, studied the crowd, mumbled names into Felicia's ear: Reed Hellstrom sat in the back in his air force uniform, his arms crossed over his Jack La-Lane chest, looking puffed up with duty. Monica Gallegos (black suit, red lips) quietly wept in a pew next to Anna Lipscomb (black suit, no lips). Liz Weston, the ornithologist, sat near them, clothbound and uncomfortable in clothes not designed by LL. Bean. Emil Pugh slumped in a far corner, smiling, as if he was thinking of hauling Field's body back to his laboratory. No sign of Doc Slagg, but he'd kept saying he and Field weren't close. I recognized a couple of others from passing them in the Biology

Department, and a couple of women from my visit to Amber Field's house. No sign of Amber yet.

Then I got a surprise. Coming through the door, shuffling and sweating, came beady-eyed Sammy Flick.

"Look who's here."

Felicia was still steaming about Etta Dangler, but that evaporated when she spotted Flick. She immediately hustled over to him.

I let my eyes roam the mourners, found Etta Dangler staring at me with something like smoky lust in her eyes. I quickly looked away, looked back. She smiled, enjoying my discomfort.

The room buzzed, and I turned toward the door, to see Amber Field coming down the aisle. No mistaking her, even though she'd concealed herself in widowhood. She wore black head to toe: a loose-fitting gown, black stockings, old-lady shoes, even a wide-brimmed black hat draped in netting that covered her face. She looked like a grim lamp shade.

She seemed a little unsteady as she walked to the front of the room. A couple of her sympathetic female friends walked along beside her, ready to make a catch if she stumbled. I gave her a nod as she passed, but she didn't acknowledge it, if she saw it at all.

Felicia returned, plopped into the pew beside me.

"What'd Sammy say?" I whispered.

"Just making an appearance for the company. They thought it would be good form, since Field died on their land. But you can bet Sammy knew the media would be here. Good chance for him to protest their innocence."

"Little weasel."

"Exactly."

The service was mercifully short, with no sermonizing. Field held no church affiliation, science being his religion, and Amber had tapped someone other than a minister to give the eulogy. The slight man had thinning, close-cropped blond hair and muttonchop sideburns. He identified himself as Stan Jones, a biologist with the U.S. Fish and Wildlife Service, and said he'd once roomed with David Field at Cornell. Jones admitted he and Field hadn't been that close in recent years, but you could tell he was honored to have been chosen to talk about what a bronze god of a scientist his former roomie had been.

Seemed to me Amber had gone sort of far afield to find a eulogist, but then, everyone said Field had few male friends. And Amber was probably afraid to pick a woman, afraid of what people would say, afraid whatever they might say could be true.

Amber wept quietly through the service, reaching up under her veil to dab her eyes with a white hankie. No wailing. No throwing herself at the casket. Dignified. Got to admire that.

I found myself having some feeling toward David Field, too. Not admiration exactly—though by all accounts he was brilliant. Most everybody also said the guy was a rat. But nobody deserves to get murdered, and I felt moved by Jones's talk of how Field's candle was snuffed before he'd had a chance to shine brightly.

Because it was a closed-casket service, we didn't have to troop past and stare at how "natural" Field looked. Since there was no graveside service, we didn't have to march to our cars and parade across town with our headlights on. In fact, Jones had to resort to "Thank you all for coming" to show us the service was over.

Felicia headed outside to give directions to her photographer in the parking lot. I stood, stretched inconspicuously, and waited a second for some blood to seep back into my pew-flattened butt. Then I trudged over to pay my respects to the widow.

Amber Field had lifted the veil back from her face to do a better job of attacking her tears. She looked haggard and gaunt, with hollows in her cheeks. Her eyes were like two holes burned in a blanket.

"Mrs. Field, I just wanted to tell you how sorry I am."

She turned away from me, said to the woman beside her, "Paula, walk me to the limousine."

Maybe she didn't hear me? Maybe she couldn't see me standing right in front of her?

"Mrs. Field?"

She shot me a look filled with anger and pain, so startling that I stepped backward and let them pass. What was that about? I was working my tail off, trying to find out who killed her husband. Then she gives me a look like that, like I was somehow responsible for her grief.

I shook my head to clear it. Her reaction must just be part of her grieving process, some kind of transference. Maybe it's easier to be angry than it is to be sad.

The chapel was full of traps. Amber Field suddenly hated me. Etta Dangler stood two pews away, talking with some woman but watching me. Sammy Flick scurried around the edges of the room. I had to get out of there. I marched up the aisle without looking right or left and went out into the hot sunshine.

I saw Felicia talking to a tall, bearded guy with cameras hanging all over him like Christmas tree ornaments. I turned away, not wanting to get in another discussion with her and certainly not wanting accidentally to get into a photo that would make it into the newspaper. I skirted the building, sticking close to the shrubbery, and practically walked up Liz Weston's back when I turned the corner.

She stood in the shadow of the building, smoking a cigarette, which seemed incongruous for someone who could be on the cover of *Outdoors* magazine. I startled her, appearing so close behind, and she dropped the butt and squished it with her black patent pump.

"Mr. Mabry. You caught me out here smoking behind the building like a schoolgirl."

"It's still legal in this country. Barely."

"I know, but I quit years ago. I'd hate for anyone to see me."

"So what's got you worshiping the bitch goddess Nicotine?"

She frowned.

"David's death, I suppose. Soon as I heard about it, I bought a pack of Camels, and I've been eating them ever since."

"It's been a shock for everyone."

Liz Weston nodded, still frowning, as if she was thinking hard about something just beyond her understanding.

"Have you determined who did it yet?" she asked. That was the question on everyone's lips, the one question I couldn't answer.

"No. I mean, I've got suspicions, but no proof."

"Just like in science," she said. "Observation is the key. Watch the creatures, study their habits. Before long, one of them will do something to prove your theory."

"I hope you're right."

She let her eyes roam over my face, searching for signs of intelligence. I tried a winning smile, but it didn't seem to help. She sighed.

"None of us will feel right about this until justice is done. Every time I think about going out in the field, I start feeling afraid. That's not like me."

I felt sure that was true. She seemed the kind of woman who's only comfortable sitting alone by a campfire or in a blind, watching birds, miles from traffic and fashion and convention. She shrugged uncomfortably against the padded shoulders of her black dress.

"I should go," she said. "I've got work to do."

"Have you started going through Field's papers yet?"

"No. Anna Lipscomb doesn't want anybody looking through his research. I think she's planning to do it herself."

"How convenient."

"What's that supposed to mean?"

I gave her a quick rundown of how Lipscomb had tried to discourage me from investigating Tierra Verde, about the behind-the-scenes pressure being exerted by Tommy Greene.

"That doesn't surprise me," she said when I was done. "The one thing Lipscomb worries about more than research is keeping the bigwigs happy. They're the ones with the money."

"Still, doesn't it seem odd to you? I mean, what's Tommy Greene trying to hide?"

She looked past me, toward the volcanoes on the western horizon. I could tell she'd rather be out there than talking to me or thinking about Field.

"I don't know what anybody's trying to hide," she said finally. "I don't understand people. Never have. Guess that's your job."

She said good-bye and tromped off toward her Land Rover. Sorting out the people and their motives was my job all right. But I wasn't sure I understood them any better than Liz Weston.

EIGHTEEN

I DON'T KNOW IF I WAS MOVED by the faraway look in Liz
Weston's eyes or if I was just sick of talking to people, but
an hour later found me out in the desert, near the murder
scene.

The place was surprisingly easy to find. For one thing,
a road existed where none had before. I'd been prepared to
make my way overland once the pavement ended, but a
graded dirt road had appeared at the spot where Erndow
and his deputies had driven me into Rio Rancho the day
we recovered the body. The new road skirted the north end
of the volcanic mesa, playing to the dips and rises in the
land rather than fighting against them. It was lined on either
side by surveyor's stakes flapping little orange flags. I followed the road toward the Rio Puerco until I could see the
dust kicked up by the construction machinery—two bulldozers, a grader, and pickups filled with equipment—then
I turned off the road and bounced over scrub and stones
until I spotted the arroyo where David Field had parked his
Jeep. The two juniper trees squatted where they had before,
but there was no sign of the blind or the Jeep. Taken away
for evidence, I supposed.

I knew I was trespassing by coming onto Tierra Verde
land, but I figured I'd take my chances. I needed some time
to think, some isolation. This certainly was a good place
for it.

I sat in the Ram with the windows rolled down, munching a submarine sandwich I'd purchased on the way over and sipping a Pepsi. My blazer lay on the seat beside me, its carnation wilting in the heat.

The construction crew was bound to have seen me, but nobody came running over to warn me against trespassing. Maybe they thought my truck was part of the crew, maybe a big boss out to monitor their work. Whatever, they seemed hard at it when I watched them through the binoculars I keep under the seat. Usually when you see a road crew, several guys are standing around, leaning on shovels and jawing. Not these guys. They worked as if a deadline loomed over their shoulders, as if the sun weren't beating down on them and the dust weren't getting in their eyes and mouths. I was impressed. They'd have the road done in no time; then the sties would be prepared and houses would start springing up from the ground, out here in the middle of nowhere.

What had David Field been doing out here? Surely, if he'd picked this lonely spot for his research, he must've known Tommy Greene's rumbling bulldozers were on the way. Why bother to start a research project in a place that would soon become a suburb?

I'd parked on a high spot above the arroyo, and I used the binoculars to scan across the place where I'd found his body. Nothing there, as far as I could see. I could make out the smudged spot where the fire had been, but the place where Field's body had lain was in the shade of the juniper and just looked dark. I thought about walking over there, but what if blood still dappled the ground? What if seeing it brought back the mental picture of Field's mutilated face? I didn't need to urp up a sandwich I'd just paid three bucks for. I watched through the binoculars, going cross-eyed, wondering what could've happened out here.

Somebody had walked right up on Field—that much was clear. Somebody coming at you with a gun, you don't wait until they're close enough to shoot. Not when you can see for miles. Maybe Field had been so engrossed in what he was doing that he hadn't seen the killer closing in. Maybe—and this was more likely—he knew the person, didn't consider him (or her) a threat.

But wouldn't he have thought that strange? Somebody he knows suddenly shows up out here? Who'd even known he was here? Anna Lipscomb said the Biology Department hadn't authorized any research at this site. Amber Field said she didn't know exactly where her husband had gone, which is why we'd hired the helicopter. Of course, she could be lying, as Erndow suspected, but I hated to think ill of a client. Maybe one of Field's many lovers had tracked him down and plugged him, but somehow that didn't seem right, either. Why come all the way out here to whack somebody?

It was possible Field provided the killer's transportation. Maybe Field brought a steamy young graduate student out to show off his research and do a little recreational humping in his duck blind. Maybe the coed got wise to what a heel the guy was and popped him.

But how had the murderous lover gotten out of here? The Jeep had been left behind, and it was a long walk to the nearest phone. Plus, the murder didn't seem to be a crime of passion. People get sloppy when they're emotionally involved.

No, Field's murder had been clean and quick. One shot in the back to immobilize him, then two in the head to make sure. It was like the professional hits I'm always reading about in the crime novels that stack up beside my bed. Bang, bang, you're dead, no witnesses, no fingerprints.

The thought of such efficiency brought me back to

Tommy Greene and Tierra Verde. Greene seemed to be a great motivator of men. Look at the way that construction crew was humping it out here in the heat. Look at the way Sammy Flick scooted around, trying to make his boss happy. And Greene clearly had power, making phone calls to university regents and Lord knows who else, trying to get one Bubba Mabry out of the picture. Meanwhile, nobody even gets to see Tommy Greene, much less confront him about the death of a biologist out here on his godforsaken land.

Tommy Greene held the key here—I was sure of that. Nothing else made sense. Of course, Tommy Greene dropping the hammer on David Field didn't make any sense, either. But it was better than nothing.

NINETEEN

I WENT SEARCHING for high ground. I wanted to watch Tierra Verde headquarters, in hope of spotting Tommy Greene, but I couldn't very well sit in the corporate parking lot. Not unless I wanted to face Bob Barron or one of the other muscle boys Greene kept around the office like knickknacks. Fortunately, the flat-roofed office building sat in something of a dip, and I found I could get a pretty good view of the place from a side street two blocks down Southern Boulevard. Unfortunately, the spot had not a speck of shade, so I sat in the heat for three hours, sweating and stewing.

For the headquarters of a booming development company, the building didn't get much traffic. I saw two vehicles—a standard Dodge four-door that looked government-issue and a battered truck full of orange construction sawhorses—come and go in the three hours I sat there. That was it. Several cars were parked behind the building, and I made them for belonging to the employees inside, but the front parking lot was kept empty for visitors who didn't come. That would change, no doubt, once Tierra Verde had houses to push on the unsuspecting public. People would drive ruts in that parking lot in search of a place to call home.

If it hadn't been so damned hot, I might've dozed off in the truck. So little to see, and I have a low threshold for boredom. I played the radio a little, but I was afraid it would sap the battery. Turning on the truck's air conditioner, even briefly, just made the heat seem more oppressive.

Finally, as the hands on my wristwatch came together on 5:25, a side door opened at Tierra Verde. I whipped the binoculars to my face, nearly poking my eyes out, and blinked until I could see a giant ducking through the doorway. It was Bob Barron, the man whose existence Sammy Flick denied. Barron looked in every direction to make sure no one was watching (ha!), then hoofed it across the parking lot to a black Buick Roadmaster parked out back. The wide car looked like an immovable mass, but it rolled after Barron cranked the engine. He pulled it up to the side entrance, where the red-haired muscle boy was holding the door. More glancing around. The goons looked like the Secret Service at work.

The redhead opened the big car's back door and stepped aside. Another man emerged into the sunlight, ever so briefly, then squeezed into the black-windowed car. A glimpse was all I got, but I could see the passenger was big and square, well dressed and swarthy. Most noticeable was his hair, which was bleached nearly white, contrasting sharply with his olive complexion—just the way Johnny Land had described Tommy Greene.

I started the Ram, and the sudden blast of hot air from the dormant air conditioner took my breath away. I waited until the Roadmaster turned west onto Southern before I swung out of the side street and followed.

We didn't go far, maybe a mile, before we were at the western fringes of Rio Rancho. The Roadmaster turned onto a street that wound away to the north. I hung back, poking along, not wanting to be visible to Barron in my big red truck.

I slowly turned onto the side street, just as the Buick disappeared over a rise a couple of blocks away. Thank goodness for rolling topography.

I crept up the hill, riding tall in the saddle, trying to see over the hill without being seen, ready to the hit the brakes and haul ass if spotted. The Roadmaster had gone down the hill and the left taillight was blinking.

From my vantage point, I could see where Barron and Greene were headed, and it made me catch my breath. A huge hacienda stood alone in the middle of a verdant lawn. The acre was surrounded by a seven-foot-tall brick wall topped by iron-work that looked like a row of spear points.

The rambling house was done in the Spanish style, white stucco topped with a red tile roof. Small windows punched holes in the stucco and the front door was a heavy wooden job that looked as if it belonged in a castle. The wide lawn was unbroken by shrubs or trees. The only interruption in the flat green grass was in back, where I could see the corner of a blue swimming pool peeking around the house, as well as the long, straight driveway that carried the Roadmaster from the street to the front of the house.

A car honked behind me, startling me. A green Ford was right on my bumper, waiting for me to finish poking over the hill. The low sun reflected on the windshield, so I couldn't see the driver, but I had a bad feeling about the car. Wasn't it similar to the one Bob Barron had driven to Felicia's? I punched the accelerator, drove past the open gate to Tommy Greene's estate as if I wasn't the least interested in it. I drove up the next hill, down the other side, the Ford no longer behind me. I turned around at a wide spot in the road and drove back toward Greene's land.

I'd been spotted, but I couldn't just get the hell out of there like a rational person. I wanted another look at Greene. I wanted some sense of what he was like, why he felt he needed the protection of thugs. I drove to his driveway and, on impulse, swung the Ram through the gate and stopped. Let him see me, what the hell. I could back out of here and be long gone before they could even get to their cars. I sat there for a minute, watching the house, no sign of any people outside, just the black Buick and the green Ford. I was thinking, Come on out of there, Greene, you coward. Let me get a look at you.

I glanced in the rearview mirror, just to be sure someone wasn't pulling into the driveway behind me, and got such a shock that I froze. A giant iron gate was whirring into place behind me, coming right out of the freaking wall, closing off my escape route. I thawed out, threw the Ram into reverse, but it was too late. There wasn't room to squeeze through, and the heavy gate looked like I could crash the truck into it all day long to no effect.

I shifted back to park, then scrambled out of the truck just as the gate clanged shut. I searched the walls for a button or a switch box that would make the gate open again. Nothing.

I heard gravel crunching at a distance behind me and whirled around. Barron and the big redhead were sprinting toward me, their suit jackets flapping, pistols in their hands.

I made this calm observation: "Oh shit! Oh Christ!"

I didn't want to leave the Ram there, but better the truck getting damaged than me. I stepped back from the wall, got a running start, and jumped. I caught hold of two of the spear points on top of the wall, tried to pull myself up. The wall was thick and the spear points were set in the middle of it; my wrists were bent and I couldn't get the oomph I needed. My feet scrabbled against the slick bricks, finding no purchase.

"No!" I screamed at the stalwart wall. "Shit!"

Then hands were on me, pulling at my clothes, big strong

hands that I knew were connected to big strong guys who were about to give me the thrashing of my life.

"Aw, hell."

I let go, landed on my feet, tried to turn around to do some quick talking. Something popped my jaw and my head jerked back, and all I saw was blue sky. Night fell suddenly, pitch-black dotted with stars, and sleep seemed like a good idea.

TWENTY

I CAME TO IN A DIM ROOM, flat on my back on somebody's bed. My jaw ached, and I explored it with my hand, rocking it back and forth on its hinges. Not broken, but swollen into a knot just to the left of my chin. I carefully flexed my limbs, searching for broken bones, afraid of what I might find. Nothing busted, though I had some sore ribs, tender to the touch, where somebody apparently had kicked me.

All in all, I was in pretty good shape for someone caught by a couple of bodybuilders. Lucky, I guess, that I got knocked cold with the first punch. They probably just circled me, nudging and sniffing like a couple of Dobermans around a possum.

I carefully sat up on the bed, swung my feet to the floor. A few aches and pains, a certain stiffness, but nothing more, really, than what somebody my age might experience sleeping off a three-day drunk.

The room was fairly bare, as if Greene kept it that way for the occasional unconscious trespasser. Just a bed, a dresser with empty drawers, and a framed photo of the Empire State Building on the wall. There was just one window, blocked by burglar bars. I tried the door, but it was locked, as expected. Nothing to do but sit and wait and wish for a bathroom.

I didn't have long to wait. I'd just sat and crossed my legs against the pressure in my bladder when the doorknob clicked and the door swung open. I hadn't even had a chance to make up a decent story.

Bob Barron's bulk filled the doorway. It hurt to meet his eyes. He seemed to be working hard to control his anger. His hands clenched into fists beside him, and he made a visible effort to open them and relax them. I didn't like that any better. We knew what a punch from him would do to me, but who knew what he could do with those thick fingers? I'd rather sleep through a beating than watch him poke holes into my internal organs.

Better start talking. "Let me explain—"

"Shut up."

Maybe talking wasn't a good idea.

"On your feet."

Okay, I could do that. No sense arguing with the man.

"Follow me."

He turned his back to me and lumbered off down a dimly lit corridor. Pretty bold. How could he be sure I wouldn't try to coldcock him from behind? Guess he figured I couldn't hurt him if I tried. Guess he was showing his contempt for me by walking away like that. Dang.

Barron stopped outside a recessed door, knocked, waited. I stopped a few feet behind him, marveling at how his broad shoulders nearly went from wall to wall in the hall.

Someone barked, "Come in," and Barron turned the knob and swung it open. He ordered me inside by tilting his head slightly, and I slipped past him and into the room, trying hard not to brush up against those bulging muscles.

The room had been built as a library, with handsome wooden shelves lining every wall. Only a few books had found their way onto them, though. Mostly, the shelves held thick slabs of paper—deeds, maybe, or lawsuits. Here and there, rolled-up blueprints stuck out at odd angles. This, I thought, is the real headquarters of Tierra Verde. And there, behind an intricately carved walnut desk, sat the man himself: Tommy Greene.

Greene wasn't wearing his suit jacket any longer, but he still had a red necktie knotted tightly around his thick neck. His blue shirt was some kind of polyester, stretched tightly across saggy breasts and an ample belly. His sleeves were rolled up to the elbow, exposing forearms the size of bowling pins. The man clearly had some age on him, but his face showed little of it, the skin pulled tautly across high cheekbones. He had a narrow, sculpted nose and dark circles under black eyes. My impression from the glimpse through the binoculars seemed accurate—the manelike pompadour of blond hair had been bleached. Dark hair showed at the roots.

I said nothing, just shoved my hands into my pockets and waited. Bob Barron loomed behind me, and I imagined I could feel his hot breath on the back of my neck.

Greene pushed some papers aside on his desk, picked up a wallet—my wallet. I hadn't even realized it was missing. He opened it, looked at the photo on my private eye's license, then up at me.

"Not very photogenic, are you, pal?" New York accent, satirical tone.

"I don't like having my picture taken."

"Me neither. We found a camera in your truck, but it didn't have film in it. Good thing for you."

Gulp.

"Now, what is it you want"—he glanced down at the ID again—"Mr. Wilton Mabry?"

"Call me Bubba."

Greene's thick-lipped mouth twitched at the corner.

"Bubba? What are you, some kinda fuckin' hillbilly?"

I shrugged. "Just a name."

"Hardly. Answer the question. What do you want?"

"I was trying to get your attention."

"You got that, pal."

"I wanted to talk to you about David Field. He was a biologist who was murdered on your—"

"I know who he was."

"Right. Of course. You've been calling people, telling them to tell me to lay off this case."

Greene leaned back in his chair, keeping his fingertips on the edge of the desk.

"Is that so? Where did you hear that?"

"I've got my sources."

"Yeah? I've got mine, too. Like, I know you were out at the construction site today, snooping around, trespassing. Then you show up here, drive right in the fuckin' gate. You got balls, pal, I'll give you that. No brains maybe. But balls, you've got."

These esteemed balls at the moment seemed to be trying to crawl up into my abdominal cavity, someplace safe from whatever beating Greene had in mind for me.

"I guess I was angry," I ventured.

"Angry? Why? Because I told people I wanted you to lay off?"

"Because you made an attempt on my life."

That had a noble ring to it. Wonder where it came from? My brain was stuck in neutral, but, as usual, my mouth was fully in gear and rolling.

Greene's eyes widened for a second.

"Is that right? Somebody tried to whack you?"

"You know it is. First, you had Beefcake here follow me to the apartment where I'm living. Then, yesterday, somebody fired three shots at me in that same parking lot. I was lucky I wasn't hit."

"Hear that, Bobby? Man thinks you tried to bump him off!"

Barron snorted behind me. I didn't turn to look. He'd already popped me once, and I didn't want to give him an excuse to do it again.

When Greene finished having himself a nice chuckle, the mirth vanished from his face and he suddenly lurched forward.

"Listen, *Bubba,* if we wanted you whacked, you'd be whacked. We don't fuck around."

"Yes, sir. Is that what happened to David Field?"

He looked me over, didn't like what he found.

"You need to learn to mind your own business, pal. Field was a troublemaker, just like you. Now he don't breathe no more."

I was having a little trouble breathing myself.

"Look, pal, don't get me wrong. We didn't kill the biologist, okay? No reason to do it. We didn't even know he was out there till the cops found him. Okay?"

I nodded, afraid to open my mouth for what might fall out.

"Now, we're tryin' to run a business here. We're tryin' to build a community out there. I've got permits to get and loans to be covered and banks and inspectors sniffing up my ass all damned day. What I don't need is some private snooper buggin' me or my people."

More nods from me.

"Am I makin' myself clear?"

"Yes, sir."

"Good. Now here's what I want you to do. I want you to turn around, walk out that door, and get in your fuckin' red truck. Then I want you to drive away and forget you ever saw me or heard of Tierra Verde or this David fuckin' Field. You got that?"

"Yes, sir."

He leaned back, nearly smiled.

"Good. Polite. I like that. You might have a goofy fuckin' name and you might pull some goddamn crazy stunt like drivin' up to my house, but I think maybe you got some sense after all. Whaddaya think, Bobby? Bubba here got some sense?"

Wincing in advance, I chanced a peek over my shoulder at Barron. Big, ugly, scary. I faced forward.

"Whatever you say, Mr. Greene."

"That's right. Whatever I say. And I say Bubba here ain't gonna cause no more problems. Right, Bubba?"

"Yes, sir."

"Good answer." He picked up my wallet again, flipped it across his desk at me.

"Pick it up and get out of here."

I did as I was told. Barron stayed hard on my heels all the way to the truck. Then I was behind the wheel, turning the key. Barron had to step back to keep from getting sprayed by the gravel the truck kicked up.

TWENTY-ONE

EXCEPT FOR A STOP AT a Giant station for a quick pee and a cold can of Pepsi to hold against the knot on my chin, I went straight home. As if I wasn't feeling sore and shamed and demoralized enough, I found a message from Amber Field on the answering machine.

"Mr. Mabry, this is Amber Field. It's two in the afternoon on Wednesday. I'm just calling to tell you I no longer require your services. Stop working on your investigation immediately. Mail me a bill. Bye."

I slumped onto the sofa, staring at the machine on the end table like it had done me wrong. Why would Amber suddenly back off? Had I failed her somehow? She didn't even know the pains I'd taken on her behalf. Maybe I should've reported my progress (or lack thereof) to her more often. I'd been trying to stay out of her way, letting her grieve. Maybe it was just a misunderstanding.

I snatched up the phone and dialed her number, listened to it ring ten times.

Damn. I didn't want to drop the case, despite my promise to Tommy Greene that I would. I felt like I might be getting close to something, might be getting deep enough into Tierra Verde and the personality of David Field that a solution to the murder would occur to me. Sure, I didn't have a true suspect yet, or a motive, but things were happening;

I was shaking things up. Now, without a client, I had no reason to go forward.

Had Tommy Greene gotten to Amber Field somehow? Had he warned her to get me out of his platinum hair? But she'd called while I was out in the desert, well before Bob Barron clipped me on the chin and dragged me into Greene's house. And before that, she'd been at her husband's funeral. Maybe Greene called her the day before. Maybe that explained why she'd acted so weird at the funeral. But, if that was the case, why didn't she just tell me then that I was fired? It would've saved me several hours in the heat and this big old knot on my jaw.

I still sat on the sofa, staring at the floor, my empty Pepsi can in my hand, when Felicia arrived. She blew through the door, then pulled up short when she saw me.

"What's the matter with you? Is that guy in the parking lot again?"

I shook my head.

"No, nothing like that. Amber Field just fired me."

"Really? Oh, that's too bad, Bubba."

She joined me on the sofa. Her warm thigh pressed against mine.

"Jesus, Bubba, what happened to you?"

"Huh?"

"Your chin's all swollen. Did you fall down?"

It figured that her first thought would be that I was once again a victim of my own clumsiness.

"Bob Barron hit me on the chin."

"Bastard! Where did this happen?"

"At Tommy Greene's house."

"You were at Tommy Greene's house? You saw him?"

"Oh yeah."

"And they beat you up? Are you all right?"

"Yeah, I'll be fine. Luckily, he knocked me out on the

first punch. Otherwise, they'd still be kicking the shit out of me.''

"Knocked you out? Did you see a doctor?''

"Naw.''

"Bubba, it's not good to be unconscious. Maybe you've got a concussion. We should take you to the emergency room.''

I scooted away from her on the couch.

"No thanks. I'm fine. Really. I'm just upset because Amber Field fired me.''

Felicia got that eager shine in her eyes, the one that usually means trouble.

"So, if you're okay, then you could tell me all about Tommy Greene, the man I can't seem to meet.''

I didn't really want to discuss it. I'd made several mistakes, and I'd look like a fool. Plus, Felicia had the dangerous tendency to put things she heard in the newspaper for all to see. I didn't want Tommy Greene coming after her (or me) because she described him in one of her front-page articles.

Naturally, none of those objections fazed her in the slightest. When Felicia gets that dogged look in her eyes, you might as well roll over and give her your tender underbelly.

I told her everything, blow by blow, without any embellishment that might make me seem less of a bumbler. She sees through lies anyway. When I was done, I essentially begged her not to write anything about Tommy Greene that would lead him back to me. I didn't want to face Greene and Barron again, especially when I had no client paying me to do it.

"So, from his house and all, you think Greene's very rich?'' she asked when I was done.

"I'd say so, though it looks like new money. The house

is spanking new, but there's nothing in it, you know? No mementos, no trophies, no family pictures. One photo of the Empire State Building. I mean, I didn't see the whole house, but what I saw looked sort of naked.''

She smiled.

"Maybe he needs to get married. Then he could get lots of swell gifts for decorating his pad.''

Does this woman have a one-track mind or what?

"I didn't see any sign of women around the place," I said. "Or at his office, either, except for that one bitchy receptionist who sicced Barron on me.

"Besides, I think Tommy Greene could afford to buy his own toasters, thank you very much. Maybe he's just been too busy cutting deals and tearing up the desert.''

The smile kept teasing Felicia's mouth. I wasn't sure I liked that.

"Maybe, if he's so rich, we should invite him to *our* wedding," she said. "He'd probably get us a nice gift.''

As usual, it took me a second to realize she was joking. She was trying to cheer me up, but it felt like she was yanking my chain.

"Yeah," I said finally. "His and hers matching coffins.''

TWENTY-TWO

I WAS SOUND ASLEEP when the doorbell rang the next morning. I responded by rolling over and snuggling deeper into the covers. The bell rang again, bringing me to consciousness, but I made no move for the door. I was naked, sleepy, clientless, forlorn. It was no time for an encounter with a door-to-door salesman or a Jehovah's Witness. *Bing-bong.* Go away. *Bing-bong.* Damn.

I creaked out of bed, cast about for something to cover my nakedness, settled on Felicia's fluffy pink robe. One size fits all. I pulled it on as I stalked toward the door. *Bing-bong.* The robe was tight across my shoulders and barely tied together in the front, but it would do long enough for me to throw somebody down the stairs, and then I could go back to sleep. *Bing-bong.*

I flung open the door, to find two guys in sunglasses staring at me. They looked like they'd been stamped out of the same mold at the Unsmiling Guys in Dark Suits Factory. Same conservative haircut, same square jaw, same chin cleft, same athletic build. Maybe I was seeing double. Maybe that crack to the jaw had done me more damage than I'd thought.

Then one of them opened his mouth, breaking the mirror-image spell: "Wilton Mabry?"

"What?"

"Federal agents." He flipped open a wallet, flashed a

star-shaped badge, flipped it closed again. "We need to talk."

I yawned in his face. Unintentionally—really.

"I was asleep."

"You seem to be awake now. May we come in?"

I thought about asking to see a warrant. I thought about slamming the door and heading for the nearest window. I thought about how I looked wearing a woman's fuzzy bathrobe. But I stepped out of the way and let them enter. You don't mess with the feds. A requirement for service in federal law enforcement is the surgical removal of the sense of humor. You can't clown around with them. Try it and there's a good chance you'll find yourself at Leavenworth, making big rocks into gravel.

The agents swept into the apartment, looking everything over as if they expected terrorists to be hiding behind the sofa. The one who seemed capable of speech asked me to sit. The other one peeked into the bedroom and around the corner into the bathroom to make sure I wasn't harboring fugitives.

I sat on the sofa, tucked the robe around my bare knees. I would've been a lot more comfortable with this intrusion if I'd been wearing pants. As it was, I felt vulnerable and stupefied. What could they want with me? What had I done? What time was it? Where was Felicia?

"Mr. Mabry," said the talking agent, "we have information that you went yesterday to the home of a Tommy Greene in Rio Rancho."

Whoa. How'd they know? I nodded, too nervous to speak.

"What's your interest in Mr. Greene and his company?"

How to sum that up? I didn't want to give too much away, but since I didn't know what they wanted, I wasn't sure which way to jump.

"I've been investigating the death of a biologist named David Field," I said. My voice sounded funny in my own head—the result of sleep or anxiety; I wasn't sure which.

"Yes?"

"Field was killed on land owned by Greene's company, Tierra Verde. So I thought there might be a connection."

"A connection to what, sir?"

I wished he would at least remove the sunglasses. I felt as if I were talking to the Terminator. His lips barely moved when he spoke and he sat up straight as Lieutenant Erndow. What they call a military bearing. I don't know where they get that. I was in the military. I try to sit up like that, I can't breathe.

"A connection between Field trespassing out there and someone knocking him off. I mean, I thought maybe Greene or one of those big goons he keeps around was the killer."

"Do you have reason to believe that's the case?"

Now we were getting into slippery areas. Federal agents like facts. Hunches, suspicions, guesses, I had plenty of, but facts? Those, I didn't have.

"One of Greene's men followed me home the other day." There, that was a fact. I had a witness.

"And?"

"My girlfriend ran him off."

His mouth tightened ever so slightly. Dang. I hate to be the source of amusement for an automaton.

"Then, the next day, somebody tried to shoot me out here in the parking lot."

One brown eyebrow appeared over the edge of the black sunglasses.

"Really. Three shots. I had to hide in the bushes."

The eyebrow disappeared.

"You reported this to the police?"

"Uh, no."

"Why not?"

"I didn't have any proof, and I didn't want the police involved. They already made it clear they didn't want me nosing around in Field's murder."

"But you persisted."

"I had a client who was paying me to do it."

"Paying you well enough to risk your life?"

"No, probably not. But that's beside the point. I didn't know I was risking my life when I took the case. And now, well, now I don't have a client at all."

The eyebrow again.

"I got fired," I confessed. "I got the message late yesterday, after I went to Tommy Greene's place."

"Too bad." He didn't sound sincere.

"That's why I was sleeping in. I'm officially unemployed at the moment."

The other agent still hovered somewhere behind me. I pulled the robe together tighter over my chest, as if I was afraid he'd get a peek at my cleavage.

"So," the talker said, "you have no reason to bother Mr. Greene further?"

"No, I guess not. But hey, while we're on the subject, it wasn't like I was the only one doing the bothering. Somebody shot at me. Bob Barron whammed me on the chin"— I pointed out the bruise on my jaw—"and they kept me locked up in Greene's house until I came to. That's kidnapping, isn't it?"

"Depends," he said. "If you were trespassing, they might be within their rights."

"Oh, never mind. Why are you guys so interested in Tommy Greene anyway?"

"Who said we are?"

"You did. You wanted to know why I was bothering

him. Now you know. I'm finished bothering him. Tell me what's going on.''

The agent got to his feet. I winced, thinking I'd pushed a little too hard. Maybe it was time for the rubber hoses.

"I'm sorry, but that's classified," he said brusquely. He looked beyond me to the other agent. "I think we're done here, don't you?"

I guess the other guy nodded, because they both headed toward the door.

"Thank you for your time, Mr. Mabry. We'll see ourselves out."

The door opened and closed before I could gather my skirts and follow. I sank back onto the sofa.

The feds. What was that all about? Were they investigating Tommy Greene? Maybe they had his place under surveillance. Maybe that's how they knew I'd been there. But why?

I shambled into the kitchen, found that Felicia had left half a pot of coffee. I poured myself a cup. I sat at the kitchen counter, sipping the hot, stale brew and thinking. It took a while, but something finally clicked. The badge the fed flashed was a five-pointed star—not an FBI badge, but the kind carried by the U.S. Marshal's Service. The marshals did a lot of different duties, most of them centered around courthouse security and the like, but part of their job was to run the federal Witness Protection Program.

Whoa.

The bad dye job, the tight skin, the sculpted nose, the tight security.

Tommy Greene was a protected witness, hiding out from somebody. It was the only explanation.

Excitement burbled in my chest. How could I confirm such a thing? They'd have the lid screwed down tight. Does it have anything to do with David Field's death? Maybe

Field found out who Greene really was and threatened to expose him. But what would a research biologist be doing with such information? And why would he care?

I felt dizzy. I needed more coffee, a shower, a shave, some pants. A smart guy probably would have listened to the feds and gone back to bed. I had no client, no reason to pursue it further. But I'm often not a smart guy, even when I try to be. Stubborn, but not always smart.

TWENTY-THREE

AMBER FIELD STILL WASN'T answering her telephone, but I spotted her white Nissan hatchback in her driveway when I drove past. I found a shady spot to park and walked back half a block to ring her bell.

I wasn't real sure what I was doing here. Usually when I'm fired, I shrug it off, sleep in for a few days, then start searching for a new client. But usually I get fired when I'm making no progress whatsoever. This time, I felt as if I'd been earning my retainer, and I didn't want to give up the case without a fight—or at least an explanation.

I watched through the sunporch to see whether Amber Field would answer the bell. The interior door swung open. Amber looked startled to see me, gulping like a guppy for a second before she got herself under control and opened the outer door.

"Mr. Mabry."

"Good morning, Mrs. Field."

Amber looked better than she had at the funeral the day before. She'd hidden the circles under her eyes with makeup and she wore her long hair pulled back with a white bow. Other than the bow, she still wore black, but the outfit was black jeans and a patterned blouse. She looked as if she was just being fashionable rather than in mourning. She'd lost weight over the past week. Gaunt and a little wrung-out, but improving.

Since she just stood there in the doorway, staring at me, I said, "May I come in? I'd like to talk to you for a minute."

The idea seemed to make her edgy.

"Didn't you get my phone message?"

"Yes, ma'am. You fired me, and that's fine. I was hoping you could tell me why."

She glanced around the porch, but apparently she couldn't see any excuse not to talk to me.

"Did you bring me your bill?"

"Yes, ma'am." I slipped the paper from my hip pocket. One thing I've learned over the years: When you get fired, get your money right then. You can get awful hungry waiting for a check in the mail.

"Come on in."

She backed away from the door, not taking her eyes off me. What was she afraid of? I was one of the good guys. I was beginning to think she'd slipped a cog. She wouldn't be the first to go crazy with mourning. Look at my mother. She never got over the sorrow and embarrassment of her father panicking and taking a dive out that hotel window. No wonder she went nuttier than a pecan log all those years later.

I followed Amber into the living room. The curtains were drawn and the lights were off, but I found my way to the sofa and sat down.

She looked too anxious to sit. She stood in front of me, too close for comfort, and held out her hand for the bill. I handed it over and she went to get her purse.

"I was hoping you'd tell me why you want me off the case," I called after her.

Her movements were jerky as she opened the purse, fished around for her checkbook. She didn't flinch when she opened the bill and saw that my services totaled seven hundred dollars. I took that as a good sign.

She paused before writing the check, looking up at me suddenly, as if she'd just heard what I'd said a full minute earlier.

"I don't want to talk about it," she said. "I just decided to let the police handle the investigation."

Amber started writing out the check, which, after all, was why I was there, but I couldn't stop asking questions.

"Did Tommy Greene contact you?"

"Who?"

"Tommy Greene, or somebody else with a company called Tierra Verde? Did they tell you to back off?"

"I've never heard of these people."

"They own the land where your husband was—"

"I really don't want to talk about this."

"I know, but I just want to ask you a couple more questions. Then I'll be on my way. Do you know anything about the federal Witness Protection Program?"

She blinked at me, not following my drift.

"Did your husband know any criminals? Or have any dealings with Tierra Verde?"

Her face clenched. This was going badly.

"Don't talk about David. You'll only make me mad. Of course David didn't associate with criminals. What a ridiculous idea."

"I'm just trying to get to the bottom—"

"If you want to know the truth, Mr. Mabry, that's why I took you off the case." She scribbled furiously on the check, ripped it out of the book as if she was pulling out my hair. "You deal in dirt. You dig around in people's lives and come up with ugly stuff, then expect that to be the answer to your questions."

"But—"

"I don't like dirt, Mr. Mabry. I don't like gossip, and I don't want my husband's name soiled after he's gone."

She stood up, briskly crossed the room, and thrust the check into my face. I took it, checked the amount, stuffed it in my shirt pocket.

"I'm sorry you feel that way," I said. "But it's my job. To find out who committed a murder, you've got to see *why* they'd do it. That means looking into the victim's life for a reason."

She shook her head while I spoke.

"No, no. I don't want that. I don't want you poking around in David's life anymore. Leave it to the police."

Two red spots burned on her cheeks like stop signs, warning me to quit pursuing it. But I couldn't.

"But Mrs. Field, at least let me tell you what I've found."

"No. I don't want to hear your dirt. Forget the whole thing."

"But you've paid me to—"

"I don't care about the money. Keeping you on retainer was a bad idea. I should've done this the day you found David's body."

"But at least—"

"No. No more. I'd like you to leave now."

What could I do? I rose, shaking my head, began moving toward the door.

"If I could ask just one more question—"

"Get out."

TWENTY-FOUR

ONCE, WHEN I WAS A BOY, two alleged friends named Junior and Norton got me lost in the woods. This was before Mama saw Jesus, before my father vanished from our lives, when the only things I had to worry about were making friends and playing in the silty dirt around our Mississippi home. Norton and Junior both were older than I was by a year or two, and they thought it would be fun to take me for a "hike" in the woods, then run off and leave me.

I'd been flattered by their attentions. They were both snaggletoothed, freckle-faced, slow-witted hillbilly boys, but because they were older, it seemed important to prove to them my worth as a woodsman. We tromped through the thick pine forest for hours, until I was far from familiar territory. Then, while I was trying to catch a crawdad in a creek, they disappeared. I turned around, to find myself all alone in a forest filled with shadows and noises and loss.

I called their names. I cried. I wandered in circles. Finally, using the sun as my guide, I trooped off on my own, in the direction I thought would be home. It was nearly dark before I ran up onto our high porch, into Mama's waiting arms.

Looking back, getting lost might've been a pivotal moment for me. It was my first taste of the abandonment to come. It was the first time so-called friends had done me wrong. (I learned later the two older boys had followed me all the way home, slipping from tree to tree, snickering at my whining.) It was the first time I saw that a fellow has to make it on his own, that he can't count on other people. And, though I didn't recognize it at the time, it probably was the first sign of the gullibility I'd inherited from my mother's side of the family.

You'd think, with my history, I'd *expect* to be abandoned in the forest. But my congenital credulity works against me. I start thinking my clients and I are on the same team, that I'm truly doing something to help while also proving my own worth. Then I get fired or fooled, and I'm reminded of how easy it is to deceive me, how hard it is to trust. Amber Field's strange behaviour reminded me once again: Got to be careful who leads you into the woods.

These thoughts hounded me all the way home. I stopped by the bank to deposit Amber Field's check, telling myself it was all over. I could stop worrying about David Field and Tommy Greene and Lieutenant Erndow and the feds. Go home, get some rest, start concentrating on the wedding, which was only three days away. I suppose I'd focused on the murder case to keep my mind off the impending Holy Matrimony. Talk about being led into the woods.

Sometimes during the past few weeks, I'd gone hours without thinking about the chance I was taking by getting married. Then realization would hit with theatrics worthy of Cecil B. DeMille. Inside my head, thunder rolled, cymbals crashed, and the Question arose like the voice of God: What the hell are you doing?

That question came up a lot in my everyday life and, invariably, the answer was, I don't know. Most of the time, I fumble along without any sort of master plan. The thing about making mistakes is, you don't know they're mistakes until it's too late. Mistakes sneak up on you; then you suffer the consequences and mop up the mess and hope you've learned something so you can avoid future mistakes. But you haven't. Because it'll be something completely different next time.

Even when given time to ponder a big decision, I can screw up royally—because things change, sometimes overnight. You commit to seeing something through, and then suddenly your client transforms from grieving widow to vicious bitch and fires your ass. For example.

Now here I am, about to take the biggest step of my life, possibly right off the edge of a cliff. And there was no way to know ahead of time. There's a reason they call it "taking the plunge." You take a deep breath, hit the water, and hope you survive the swim.

Let's face it: The odds are not in our favor. Felicia and I are two people in our thirties, each getting married for the first time. We've developed our own idiosyncratic lifestyles and have grown more or less comfortable being alone. Felicia had her share of hit-or-miss romances but never clicked with the right guy. I've heard more of the details than I care to remember. And me? I was a skirt hound for years. I bedded down anything with a pulse, then tried to slip away before sunrise. No commitments, no entanglements.

All around us, we watched our contemporaries fall into desperate marriage-and-divorce cycles, and the idea of giving it a try had pretty much gone south for each of us.

Then we met, crossing paths while we separately sought the living Elvis. I thought she was the testiest little witch I'd ever encountered. She thought I should be whittling outside a gas station somewhere rather than trying to pretend I was a private eye. It was true love.

It took awhile to see it. At first, Felicia and I were antagonists, competing over the same goal. Then, during the course of the Elvis investigation, we began to work together. When it was all over, we had a solid business reason—writing the book—for keeping each other's company. By the time the book sank without so much as a ripple, we were lovers, living together at the Desert Breeze, as intertwined as chiles on a *ristra*.

I know the moment when everything changed. It's one of those sparkling moments that have been all too rare in my life.

Felicia had come to the Desert Breeze to work with me on the book. She'd awakened me, ordered me to get dressed, and put me to work. I paced around the room, slurping coffee and thinking out loud while Felicia hammered at a typewriter. It was early, not long after dawn, and the sunlight streamed through the smudged window, spotlighting Felicia, who sat in a haze of cigarette smoke. We were arguing about something, some picayune "who did what" point in the adventure we were putting on paper. Felicia's cheeks were flushed with annoyance and her eyes flamed, but the way the sunbeam lit her pale skin made me catch my breath.

She caught me looking.

"What? Why are you staring at me like that?"

I couldn't answer, not truthfully anyway. Because I knew at that moment I was in love with her. Here we were, in the middle of an argument, proving once again how pigheaded we both could be, but I knew. We hadn't even kissed at that point, hadn't touched more than the brushing of shoulders, the accidental lingering of hands. But I knew.

The sudden knowledge caused me to break out in a sweat and go stupid. Should I tell her? Should I act on this feeling? Should I do nothing and see if it passes in a few days, like the flu?

She watched me as I had this attack of the blithers. Her

expression softened. The fire in her eyes dipped to a romantic fireplace flicker. Then I knew that she knew it, too.

Typical of us, we didn't act on it right away. The moment was broken by twitches and the clearing of throats. Felicia said something about how we'd better get back to work. But the argument had died, and something new and unwieldy had sprung up in its place.

After that, Felicia slowly infiltrated every part of my life. I'd been a solitary man, cut off from my family and my past, living in virtual anonymity on the fringes of the Cruise. I had friends and flings, but no one I really trusted, no one who really cared.

My life began to orbit around Felicia. I'd begun to feel as if my destiny wasn't to become a famous private investigator, but to be the man behind Felicia's successes. I could live with that. It's not as if I have strong ambitions that can't be superseded for the woman in my life. Maybe my role is to listen as she describes how her editors ruined her day, then say, "Dirty bastards!"

We're all looking for a place to fit, an anchor for our lives, a home. Once you have one, it defines the roles you play, the acts of your life. The problem with marriage is, you're making a vow never to bring down the curtain.

The only thing I feared worse than the wedding ceremony itself was the thought that somehow the marriage wouldn't work out, that I'd altered my life to accommodate Felicia and then suddenly she wouldn't be there. It's not that I didn't trust her. It was myself who worried me.

I recognize that constant contact with me can be aggravating. Felicia might get fed up with me. I might run her off. Or I might be the one who strays. Look at how my libido shifted into overdrive during my flirtfest with Etta Dangler. Worse yet, I might just vanish into anonymity again.

That was the example that was set for me. When the going got weird back home, my dad disappeared. He hadn't been there much anyway. My father was also named Wilton Mabry, though he was known as ''Dub'' in truck stops all over America. Dub spent three weeks out of every month hauling produce or furniture or frozen fish up and down interstate highways in his big red Kenworth. When he was home, he spent most of the time behind closed doors with Mama.

I was nine when Jesus let Mom down and all the newspapers made fun of her. But I was old enough to see how Dub carried his shame around town, how his trips away grew longer. Then he just stopped coming home. Never even said good-bye.

I hated him for it. Mama already was brittle and frail. She needed him, and he abandoned her—and me. He left me there to watch her crumble and rebuild into a new, more zealous Mama, who sang hymns while cleaning and often sat up late into the night, drinking coffee and muttering, waiting on Jesus to reappear.

Nine-year-olds thrive on vows and pledges and blood brotherhood. They're always testing to see how long promises last. I made myself a vow: If I ever had a wife and family, I'd never forsake them. It was one life vow I never broke, because I never gave myself the opportunity. I avoided relationships, danced away when women got too involved with me. Why test a perfect record?

While that reluctance to commit was a part of Dub's legacy, the opposing part was a certain doggedness that had helped me through many scrapes. I'm no quitter. I get hold of something, and I take pride in not letting go. Which made wedding vows all the more daunting. What if I got into it, then realized I'd made a mistake? Would I walk away, or would I fight for every scrap of the relationship until nothing was left but bones and bitterness? Could I be loyal and tenacious enough to make it thrive? I know feelings can be fickle as the flip of a coin. For all my vows and striving and stubbornness, I honestly had no idea how I would react to whatever the future might hold.

For now, I could focus on the trauma of the wedding, of getting through the event intact. But whenever I glimpsed the void beyond, fear flowed through me like ink, uncertainty clogged my veins, and dark omens seized my heart.

All of which is why losing my client hit me so hard. I needed the distraction.

TWENTY-FIVE

I'D BARELY CLEARED the apartment door when I saw the red light flashing on the answering machine. I was tempted to walk right out the door again, or to ignore the blinking beacon at least. But the message might be from Felicia. Maybe she'd decided to change all the colors at the wedding. Maybe she'd decided to call the whole thing off. I pushed the button, rewound the tape, played it back.

"I hope I have the right number. I'm looking for Bubba Mabry? This is Liz Weston. Please call me right away at my office."

She'd recited the number twice, making it too easy for me. Okay, I wouldn't just ignore the message. I'd call her, tell her I was no longer on the case, get off the phone, take a nap. Liz Weston seemed like a perfectly likable person, straightforward and dedicated to her work. But I'd had enough of her colleagues and their infighting, their back stabbing, and their superiority complexes.

She answered on the first ring. I identified myself, and I had my mouth open to explain how I'd been fired, but she didn't give me a chance.

"Mr. Mabry, I'm glad to hear from you. The department is buzzing, and I thought you should know about it."

"What happened?"

"Monica Gallegos got into a fight with one of the students today. Over David Field."

"Little late for that, isn't it? Field's no longer available."

"Wasn't that kind of a fight. This student—her name's Mary something—was sounding off about how David deserved what he got because of the way he treated women. I guess she'd slept with David; then he'd never called her, avoided her. Anyway, Monica—she's the department secretary?"

"We've met."

"Monica couldn't take any more, I guess, and she told Mary to shut up about David. She started crying, saying Mary shouldn't speak ill of the dead, even if David had been a bastard when he was alive. Next thing you know, Monica smacks her in the face and the two of them are rolling around on the floor, pulling hair, and punching and scratching."

"That must've been a sight."

"It was. Doc Slagg waded in and pulled them apart, and then Lipscomb called them to her office. They're still in there now. Everybody's talking about it."

I'll bet.

"And you're telling me this because?"

"I just thought you should know. It seemed so odd. Monica definitely has some problem with David's death to react like that. You've talked to her already?"

"Yeah. In fact, I'm through talking to people in this case."

"You know who did it?"

"Not exactly. I have some ideas, but I've got no client."

I told her how Amber Field took me off the case, and how I was glad to be shat of it.

"I'm sorry to hear that," she said glumly. "Someone needs to find David's killer."

"I guess we'll leave it to the police. That's what Mrs. Field wants."

"She's hiding something."

"What?"

"Amber. She's got something to hide. Otherwise, she wouldn't dismiss you."

"Now what makes you say that?"

"I've suspected her all along. She's a strange person. Always trying to keep up the best front, but all the while feeding her own jealousies and suspicions. If she'd been at the office today when Monica and Mary went at each other, she probably would've killed them both."

I mulled that over. Maybe I'd underestimated Amber Field. I'd thought grief was her driving emotion, but perhaps her vengeful side was stronger than I'd seen.

"Maybe you're right," I said, "but it's not my business anymore. I'm off the case."

There was a pause. I tried to think of a pleasant way to extricate myself from the conversation.

"I'll pay you," she said, and I nearly dropped the phone. "I want you to stay after this case. I'll be your client."

"Now why would you want to do that?"

"David Field was my colleague. I don't want to see his killer get away with it."

"He was Anna Lipscomb's colleague, too, but you don't see her ponying up a retainer to investigate his death. In fact, she tried to warn me away."

"I don't care about that. I...I think somebody should make sure the murder is solved. I don't want it covered up."

Something about her manner brought the dawn.

"Sure you and David weren't more than just colleagues?"

That was greeted by a healthy silence.

"See?" she said finally. "You have a way with people.

You're insightful. You're just the man to sort through it all and find David's killer."

I'd been shooting from the hip, no idea what I was saying, and I'd hit a bull's-eye.

"You're saying there *was* something going on between you two?"

"Well, not anymore. But yes, David and I were lovers at one time."

"After he was married to Amber?"

"Yeah. I'm not proud of it and it didn't last long. I'm sure that, to him, it was just another fling. But I find I still have strong feelings for him, now that he's dead. I thought I was beyond all that. But I want—how to say it? I want him *avenged.*"

Now, I'm no Masked Avenger, but it did rankle that I'd had to drop the case just when I felt as if I was getting somewhere. And I still needed a paying client, whether it was on this case or something else. I told her my fee, and she didn't balk, so I agreed to resume the investigation.

"Thank you, Mr. Mabry. I'm relieved."

She exhaled into the phone, making a rushing noise in my ear.

"You still smoking?"

"Yeah. I'm not supposed to smoke in the building, but I've got the office door closed and I'm risking it. I seem to be taking a lot of risks these days."

"Me, too."

I told her about my run-in with Tommy Greene and his thugs, my suspicions that Tierra Verde's development was somehow connected to Field's death. She'd never heard of Greene, and she didn't seem to think much of my theories.

"Now that I'm your client, I can make suggestions?"

"Sure."

"I think you should look at Amber Field. I think she

could've done it. You wouldn't imagine it to look at her, but she's got plenty of motive. David certainly could make people's emotions run high—look at the hair pulling we had down here today.''

''I don't know—''

''I mean, I know you didn't want to believe that when *she* was your client. But I think that's where the answer lies. A jealous wife, an angry lover, somebody David threw over. It fits.''

I didn't want to disappoint her, not before I'd even seen any of her money. Let her have her theories. They were certainly as plausible as anything I'd cooked up. I told her I'd look into those angles, but I still wanted to keep an eye on Tommy Greene. I said I'd be in touch, then hung up.

Well, well, well. Liz Weston and David Field had been lovers. That must've been something to see. Two well-muscled bronzed types tearing off their safari wear to tumble into bed. Must've been like two lions going at it. And she still feels strongly for him. His death drove her to take up smoking again, led her to hire me.

I had a client. Guess I wouldn't be taking that nap.

TWENTY-SIX

I MADE A FEW PHONE CALLS, but I didn't get anywhere. Johnny Land was too busy to talk to me. Monica Gallegos had been sent home for the day, and I couldn't find her home number. Lieutenant Erndow was unavailable.

Oh, well. I cracked open a beer, kicked off my shoes, and settled onto the sofa to await Felicia's arrival from work. I'd barely warmed the seat when someone banged on the door. I shambled across the carpet in my sock feet, and flinched at the static electricity shock I got from the doorknob. I swung the door open and got a bigger shock.

A black gun stared in at me. Somebody was holding it, pointing it at me—that much was clear. But, at first, all I could see was the gun. I tore my eyes away from the semi-automatic pistol and took in the arm and the rest of the man who held it. Short guy, stocky, black suit that must've been hellish in this heat. I got to his face and found thick lips and bushy black eyebrows and a nose that had been broken so many times, it looked like it was pointing back over his shoulder. His left eye had a milky glint in it, a cataract that reflected the light. Screwed down tightly on top of his head was a gray porkpie hat.

''Back inside,'' he said calmly, and I obeyed.

It was the guy in the black Chevy Cavalier who'd tailed me days before. I'd wondered what had become of him, why Bob Barron had been sent to do the dirty work instead of Porkpie here. But why would Tommy Greene sic this guy on me now? As far as he knew, I was off the case.

The man in the hat ordered me back onto the sofa and I sat. He climbed up onto one of the bar stools at the counter that separates the kitchen from the living area and sat facing me. His feet couldn't reach the footrest and his legs dangled, but the tall chair gave him the high ground.

Maybe it was time to start talking.

"There must be some misunderstanding. I told Mr. Greene I wouldn't poke around in the Field murder anymore. When he sent you here, did he—"

"He didn't send me."

"What?"

"You think I work for Tommy Greene? That's it, right? I don't. I'm Tommy Greene's worst fuckin' nightmare."

Time to reorganize my thoughts. I'd assumed the tail had been part of Greene's army of goons. If he wasn't, then just who was this guy and why was he pointing a gun at me?

I voiced these concerns, saying, "Who are you, and why are you pointing that gun at me?"

He said, "Shaddup."

Okay, that didn't work. Wait him out, then. If he'd come here to shoot me, he'd already had plenty of opportunity. The man came here to talk. If I waited, the words would come. For now, though, it looked as if he just wanted to stare at me with his good eye and size me up. I sat up straighter on the couch, tried to look like a hardened professional. Probably came across like Barney Fife.

"You're after the money, ain't ya?" he said finally.

I paused, giving proper consideration to his question before replying, "Huh?"

"The money. That's what you're after. Just like me."

"I have no idea what you're talking about."

"Don't be coy with me, pal. I saw you go out to Tommy Greene's yesterday. Saw them rough you up. You're lucky they let you walk away."

I nodded. I'd already recognized that stroke of luck.

"And I saw you before that, too. When you went to his office. You musta seen me, too, 'cause you did that nice piece of drivin' to shake me."

I almost smiled. The driving maneuver was about the only thing that had gone right for me all week.

"I wasted valuable time trackin' you down here," he continued. "But I'm here to tell ya, forget the money. It's mine."

"I honestly don't know what you're talking about."

"Then why're you tryin' to move on Tony Birbone?"

"Who?"

"C'mon, don't play stupid. Tony Birbone. Tommy Greene. You're trying to cut into my action."

I tried to follow, but the rhyming name made me think of that old song, "The Name Game." Tony, Tony, Bir-bone, banana-bana, bo-boney, fee-fi-fo-foney—

"You listenin' to me here, or what?"

"Sorry. You're going to have to explain this better. Tommy Greene's real name is Birbone?"

He rolled his eyes, sighed. Then he gave me that hard stare again, squinting the bad eye against the light. It was like being scrutinized by Popeye.

"Maybe I fucked up here," he said finally. "You're not trying to claim the reward?"

I shook my head slowly. I hesitated because this guy clearly had information I needed. I didn't want him to shoot me, but I didn't want him just to stalk out the door, either.

"I'm not competing with you," I said. "Why don't you stop pointing that gun at me and we'll talk?"

"Why don't you bite me? I point my gun where I like."

"Okay, don't get excited. I just thought we could, you know, swap information. I'm a private investigator, looking into a murder on Greene, er, Birbone's land. Maybe I've got some stuff you can use."

"Like what?"

"Well, wait a minute. Shouldn't it be a fair trade?"

"Hey, fuck you. Who's got the gun here?"

"Fine. You want to shoot me, make a big mess, get the cops hunting you, go ahead. Shoot."

What was I saying? Sure, I wanted to come across as a tough guy. I wanted this tough guy in the hat to cough up some facts about Tommy Greene. But "go ahead, shoot?" Jeez.

He studied me with that squint; then the best possible thing happened. His doughy face split into a smile.

"You think I wouldn't shoot you if the mood struck me?"

The smile emboldened me.

"Sure you would. But I got information you could use. You don't want to shoot me."

"I dunno. The temptation's pretty strong right now. My trigger finger's itching."

"You've seen too many gangster movies."

His thick eyebrows shot up at that one.

"Hey, pal, don't push it. 'Gangster movies.' Shit. I've seen the real thing every day of my life. I'm from New York, you fuckin' goober, where they got real criminals."

"Yeah? We got real criminals out here, too. Believe me, I've known a few."

"You got cowboys out here. Fuckin' small-time outlaws who rob banks and shit. That's not criminal enterprise. Real crime is big business, you know? You get a piece of the action in concrete or the garbage business or the numbers racket. You push out the small-timers and run things like a corporation. Now *that's* crime."

He seemed to be congratulating himself on this little speech, and, for some reason, I felt compelled to bring him down a notch.

"You don't look like a businessman to me."

"Did I say I was? I'm a bounty hunter."

"A what?"

"You heard me. I'm out here in this fuckin' cow town to collect the money."

It took some time to process this, especially since I didn't know what the hell he was talking about.

"And I don't want you gettin' in my way, see?"

He waved the gun as he spoke. I wished he'd put the thing down so I could concentrate.

"All right," I ventured. "Let's see if I got this straight. You want to collect a bounty on Tommy Greene, right?"

"What've I been sayin' here?"

"And you don't want me to get in your way."

"You got some kind of mental problem?"

"No, I'm just a little slow on the uptake. See, if I don't know what you're talking about exactly, how can I be sure I'm not in your way?"

He pondered this a moment.

"Maybe if you don't know what I'm talkin' about, I'm the one who's made the mistake. Maybe I shoulda just taken my chances, and if you got in the way, I'da hadta eliminate you."

"You don't want to do that. I don't want to mess up your bounty hunting, and I sure as hell don't want to catch a bullet because I'm standing in the wrong spot."

"You didn't know about the bounty?"

I shook my head.

"Then I'm gonna hafta shoot you. 'Cause now you're gonna try to beat me to it."

"No, I'm not. I don't want to take that kind of risk. I've already taken my licks from Tommy Greene's boys."

"Yeah? That what happened to your jaw?"

"That's right. It would take a lot of money to get me to go out there again."

"How about a million bucks?"

That chilled me.

"A million?"

"You heard me. And it's mine. Or it soon will be. And if you try to stand between me and that money, you're a goner."

"All right, take it easy. I told you, I don't want the money. A million, huh? Whew. No, I don't want it. Not if it means taking out Tommy Greene."

"Okay, you remember that."

"Sure, fine. Why don't you put down the gun and we'll start over?"

"Whattaya mean?"

"Let's introduce ourselves. I'm Bubba Mabry. What's your name?"

"I know who the fuck you are. You think I just blow in here without checkin' you out?"

"Then you should know I'm not after a bounty. I'm after whoever killed David Field."

"That's not what I heard about you. I heard you were hard up for dough. That you was always lookin' for a score."

"Not this time. I've got a paying client. I'm getting married in a couple of days. I don't need this right now."

"You don't need a million dollars?"

"Not this way. That's working too hard for the money, even that much money. Tommy Greene's in the Witness

Protection Program, right? You try to gun him down, you're going to have the feds all over your ass.''

He smiled.

"That just makes it more interestin'.''

"What did he do anyway, this Greene? Why is he worth a million to somebody?''

"What, you live in a cave out here? You don't read the papers? The name Tony Birbone means nothin' to you?''

I shrugged sheepishly. He cleared his throat as if preparing to lecture.

"Tony 'the Tiger' Birbone ratted out his godfather, Enrico Profundo. That name mean anythin' to you?''

"Sure. Profundo's been on the news. Wears nice suits. Got convicted recently, right?''

"Right. Profundo's doin' eight to ten in the federal slammer as we speak, and he owes it all to Tony the Tiger. Coupla years ago, Tony got caught with his hand in the cookie jar, see? He was skimming off the mob profits. When Profundo found out about it, he was gonna bump off Tony, but somebody tipped Tony and he went to the feds and offered them Profundo in exchange for a new face and a new life.''

That explained the bad dye job and the tight skin. Tony the Tiger probably picked his new face out of a magazine.

"So,'' he continued, "Tony testifies, Profundo goes up the river, and Tony vanishes into the Witness Protection Program. Profundo's not gonna take that lyin' down, right? So he offers up a million to whoever finds Tony and takes him out. Tony the Tiger becomes Tony the Target.''

"And you're going to collect the bounty.''

"That's right. And I don't need some goober private eye gettin' in my way.''

I resented the "goober'' part, but I let it pass.

"Maybe I can help," I offered. "I give you some information and you can forget you ever met me."

"Yeah? You got information you think I can use?"

"Maybe so. I've been inside Greene's house, know something of the layout. That might help."

A light came on in his good eye.

"That's not bad."

"I've been inside his office, too. You probably haven't."

"True."

"So, I help you out and you don't shoot me. We got a deal?"

He thought it over.

"Okay, pal. That's a deal. But you get in my way later, you change your mind about trying to collect the bounty, then all bets are off and your ass is mine. Got it?"

"Got it."

I told him everything I could remember about the estate and the corporate headquarters, Bob Barron and the red-haired thug, the marshals who showed up at my doorstep that morning. He tried to look bored, but halfway through my story, he set the gun on the counter—within reach, but not pointing at me anymore.

When I was done, he muttered, "Not bad. Not bad at all."

He seemed lost in thought, as if he was already planning his assault on Tommy Greene.

"Okay," he said. "I'm outta here."

"Hey, one more thing," I called as he headed for the door. "Did you shoot at me the other night?"

"What?"

"Somebody popped off a few shots at me in the parking lot Tuesday night. Was that you?"

He gave me the hard squint.

"Wasn't me, pal. I don't miss. If I wanted you whacked, you'd be whacked."

"That's what people keep telling me."

TWENTY-SEVEN

SOMETIMES I THINK the human brain is like those old eight-track tapes that came and went in the seventies. Different programs are playing on different tracks at any given time. You've got whatever you're actually doing at that moment. Maybe you've got some other problem that you're sorting out in the back of your mind. You've got a track that governs your behavior, playing back scoldings you got when you were a kid or whatever religious upbringing got thumped into your skull. And then, with me at least, there's a music track that's like the sound track of my life. Whenever my brain's at rest, some song burbles up and I'll catch myself whistling or humming snatches of it. Maybe it's a song I heard on the radio from a passing car or maybe it's something I heard years ago that suddenly, for some reason, pops up and plays.

Friday morning, the song that kept playing in my head was "The Name Game." Tony, Tony, Birbone, banana-bana, bo-boney, fee-fi-fo-foney, Tony! Over and over, until I thought I'd lose my mind.

Worse, I couldn't let it out. I couldn't sing it or hum it without giving away what I knew about Tommy Greene's secret identity. First, Felicia was around the house, puttering in the kitchen, getting ready for work. Then I went to see Liz Weston. Either of them might remember Birbone's name from the news accounts of the Profundo trial. I couldn't take that chance.

Liz Weston lived in the Monte Vista neighborhood, between the university and the cappuccino district known as Nob Hill. The house was a brown stucco job, shaded by two gnarly cottonwoods that reached long arms up over its flat roof. The dusty playground of an elementary school across the street was filled with kids enjoying recess, whooping and squealing. Some things are worse than living in an apartment complex.

She answered the door in exercise togs—an electric blue leotard and short black tights. Her sun-streaked hair was pulled back into a ponytail. Her square tan face glistened with perspiration.

"Oh, Mr. Mabry. I wasn't expecting you."

"Looks like I caught you in the middle of a workout."

"Trying to sweat the nicotine out of my system. Come on in."

I followed her inside. The house was cool and dim, with white walls and well-worn furniture. We turned a corner from the entrance hall, and I nearly jumped out of my skin. A giant mask hung on the wall, blue and red and green, its eyes protruding, its pointed tongue sticking out. It looked like someone being strangled.

Liz Weston smiled at my alarm.

"Sorry. Guess I should've warned you. It's from Bali. My dad brought it back from one of his expeditions."

"Expeditions?"

"My dad taught anthropology at UNM. This was his house before he died. Paul Weston?"

I shook my head to show I'd never heard of him.

"I suppose I'm following in his footsteps, though I'm more interested in birds than in primitive human cultures.

Still, when I'm out in the field, I sometimes pick up pot-sherds and wonder what he would've made of them.''

A vinyl mat lay in the middle of the living room floor, where Liz Weston had been doing her exercises. She toed it out of the way, offered coffee, then went toward the kitchen, toweling off her face.

I sat on the sofa and studied the mask, thinking, I know just how you feel, friend.

She appeared a couple of minutes later, still wearing the skimpy workout duds but carrying a tray with two steaming cups.

"So, how come you're here?" she asked, without making it sound like I'd disrupted her morning.

"I wanted to pick up my retainer," I said hesitantly, "and I thought I'd brief you further on what I have so far."

"Good idea. I've got some more theories, too."

I didn't want her theories; I wanted her money.

I sipped the strong coffee while she fetched her check-book. Once she wrote a check for a hundred bucks and handed it over, I felt relieved. I was officially back on the case now, plus I had another check. It might even cover the wedding champagne.

I didn't have much to tell her beyond what I'd said on the phone, but I tried to make the best of it. I'd brought with me a slim folder that contained the few notes I'd made and the stuff I'd pilfered from David Field's office.

She sat next to me, still glowing and flexing from the workout. I could feel the heat radiating from her, but I tried not to get distracted by her tawny body. I opened the folder, walked her through it one piece of paper at a time.

She cleared up a couple of things for me—translated research notes I'd found in Field's desk, told me a memo from Anna Lipscomb was purely routine. I didn't say anything more about Tommy Greene or Tierra Verde. I certainly didn't mention Porkpie or what he'd told me about the Witness Protection Program and Enrico Profundo's reward. She'd said she wasn't interested in that angle anyway, so why pursue it? I didn't want to tangle with Tommy Greene or Porkpie again. The wedding was two days away. I didn't want the ritual altered into a funeral.

I was about done with my pitiful folder of nothing when she stopped me.

"Where did you get this?"

"What?"

I'd come to the back of the file and the photograph of the burrowing owl I'd swiped from Field's office.

"This. This photo."

She studied it. It was a nice shot, as bird pictures go, close-up and crisp, showing clearly the owl's menacing yellow eyes, its long legs, and its compact brown-and-white-streaked body.

"It was in Field's desk. I meant to show that to you earlier, see if you could make anything—"

"David had this in his desk?"

"Yeah. Is it important?"

"I don't know. It's just odd he'd have such a thing. I wonder where he got it."

I opened my mouth to tell her, but she was rolling now.

"This is *Athene cunicularia mexicana,* a type of owl that lives south of here. David hadn't been doing any work in Mexico, not since I've known him. He didn't even speak Spanish. This is a rare bird, endangered. See the dark collar around its neck? That's how you can tell it from the burrowing owls that live in the desert here."

"But—"

"I wonder why he'd have a photo of this bird? Birds weren't David's specialty; they're mine. I wonder if somebody gave him this photo to add to my collection?"

"Hang on a second. You're telling me this bird doesn't live around here?"

She gave me a quizzical look.

"Definitely not. It's Mexican, lives in the southernmost reaches of the Chihuahuan Desert."

"But I've seen them."

"You what?"

"I've seen them. They're all over the place out where Field was killed."

Her eyes jerked from me to the picture and back again.

"That's not possible."

"I beg to differ. I've seen them out there twice. One of them nearly knocked me over, flew right at my head."

"And they had these dark collars?"

"Yeah, yeah. It's the same bird. That's why I took this picture from his office. I thought it might mean something. I meant to show it to you earlier."

Her eyes were wide blue pools in her brown face.

"You've got to take me there."

"No way."

"Right now."

"I don't think that would be such a good idea."

"Don't you see? This is an endangered species. If it's come this far north, that's big news for the ecological biologists."

"Huh?"

"And these birds live out there where they're going to build that new subdivision?"

"Yeah, they—"

"We've got to hurry."

She leapt to her feet, saying she'd just change clothes quickly, then disappeared into the back of the house.

What the hell? So much excitement over a bird, and an unpleasant, rattlesnake-imitating bird at that. What was I doing getting mixed up with these scientist types? Liz Weston seemed more worked up over the owls than she was about David Field.

She blew back into the room, dressed in hiking shorts and boots and a T-shirt decorated with hieroglyphics of birds. She didn't even stop as she buckled a fanny pack around her trim waist.

"Let's go."

"Are you sure we—"

"Right now," she said. "Before it's too late."

TWENTY-EIGHT

WE WERE HALFWAY to Rio Rancho before Liz Weston made me understand why some blooming owls might be important. Most people get excited, they talk fast and make it simple. Liz, like most scientists, slipped into technical jargon that I couldn't make heads nor tails of.

Ask enough dumb questions, though, and even an agitated ornithologist can get exasperated and spell it out clearly.

"Look," she said, "these birds aren't supposed to live this far north. If they've moved up here, it means the desert's moving, too."

I was pretty sure the desert wasn't going anywhere.

"I'm talking about a change in climate," she said. "Have you noticed how hot and dry it's been this summer?"

"Yeah. So?"

"And last summer was the same way?"

"Yeah, yeah, get to the point."

"You ever heard of global warming?"

"Sure, that's where—"

"If the climate is indeed warming and getting drier, that means the desert will change and expand its boundaries— fewer trees, less grass, less water. Animals move to keep close to the resources they need. These owls usually like to live in the same area year-round. If they've come up here, it's an indicator."

"An indicator?"

She sighed. I felt like the doofiest of freshmen.

"The desert's fragile, right?"

"Right."

"Up here, where the desert is mixed with mountain ranges, you get lots of different microclimates. We're on the edge, see? Animals migrate, plants die off, and pretty soon you're looking at a different ecology."

"What's this got to do with—"

"It was David's area of expertise. He studied the biomes in search of such changes."

"Biomes?"

"Never mind. Just trust me. If these birds are *mexicanas,* it's a big deal."

"They're just like the one in the picture."

"Let me judge that."

"What? I can't tell one bird from another?"

"I'm an expert, okay? How soon till we get there?"

"It'll be awhile yet. It's out in the middle of nowhere."

She pulled the photo out of the folder on the seat between us, studied it some more.

I drove in silence, letting my misgivings crawl all over me. I didn't want to go to Tierra Verde's land again. I'd been spotted last time and reported to Tommy Greene. They'd know to watch for me now, but here I go, in my big red truck, asking for trouble.

I tried to voice these concerns to Liz Weston, but she was having none of it.

"If you're scared, I'll go out there on my own," she said, and she sounded determined enough that I believed her.

"No, I'm not scared. Really. Well, maybe a little. Just

stick close to the truck when we get out there. We may have to haul ass.''

I found the dirt road at the edge of Rio Rancho and steered the Ram up the mesa and down the other side toward the Rio Puerco. The Tierra Verde crew had extended the road another half a mile, practically overnight, so the construction machinery was farther away when I parked near the arroyo where David Field had done his last bird-watching. Still, I was uneasy. They probably had cellular phones or walkie-talkies. How long would it take them to notice us and call Tommy Greene?

Liz Weston didn't seem to share these concerns. As soon as I stopped the truck, she was out the door, moving toward the owl colony in a crouch. She stopped halfway between me and the birds and produced compact binoculars from her fanny pack. It didn't take her long to see what she needed to see. I was relieved to see her stand and head back for the truck.

''You were right,'' she said as she climbed into the cab. ''They're the Mexican owls. Looks like maybe a dozen burrows.''

One of the bulldozers cranked up in the distance, its loud rumble vibrating everything for a mile around. Two owls took flight and circled, as if looking for the source of the noise.

''This whole area is to be leveled, isn't it?'' Liz Weston shouted.

''Yeah. It's all going to be a subdivision.''

''That's why David was killed.''

I couldn't have heard her right. I rolled up my window to shut out some of the construction noise.

''You want to run that by me again?''

''Don't you see? He found this colony of owls out here. It's a big discovery and they're an endangered species.''

"Yeah?"

"You can't just bulldoze over an endangered species. You have to get government approval. This project would be tied up in the courts for years."

"You think Tommy Greene snuffed Field over birds?"

"A planned community is a big investment. Greene probably can't afford any delays."

With the mob's pilfered money, he could probably afford all the delays anybody could dream up. But I suspected it would go against Greene's nature to wait.

"David must've gone to Tierra Verde and warned them about the owls," Liz speculated. "He must've told them he'd report the colony, which could scrap all their plans."

It made sense. Tommy Greene wouldn't take kindly to threats. David Field had no way to know he was dealing with a former mobster, probably didn't know how much trouble he'd stirred up until somebody pointed a gun at him.

A cloud of dust rose from the road back toward Rio Rancho. I snatched Liz Weston's binoculars away from her, focused into the distance. A green Ford roared along the road, headed our way. As it topped a rise, I could see through the open driver's side window. I looked right into the lifeless eyes of Bob Barron.

"Uh-oh."

"What is it?"

"Unless I miss my guess, that's the guy who shot your boyfriend."

"Where? In that car? I'd like to talk to him."

"Oh no you don't. We're getting out of here."

"Don't you have a gun?"

"Yeah, but I don't feel like shooting anybody today. The guy in that car wouldn't hesitate."

I cranked up the Ram, backed it away from the arroyo, and took off toward the northeast, traveling overland up the broken black battlements of the mesa. I tried to steer around as much of the scrub as possible, but tumbleweeds dragged the bottom of the truck and rocks scraped the axles.

I watched the rearview mirror, saw that Bob Barron had no problem tearing up a company vehicle. He plowed across the open country in the low Ford, throwing up dust and weeds.

"He's getting closer," Liz Weston said at my shoulder. She bounced on her knees, trying to hold on, watching out the back window.

"I'm trying not to tear up my truck."

"How do you feel about bullet holes?"

That got me to floor it. We rocketed over the bumps and dips, dodged trees and boulders. Still, Barron gained on us.

We topped a ridge, and I could see Rio Rancho's gray streets and pastel houses embroidered across the flat tan of the desert. If I could reach a street before he caught up with us, maybe I could outrun him, drive to the nearest police station.

"Whoa!" Liz suddenly yelled beside me.

"What? What?"

"I think he blew a tire."

I looked in the mirror to see the Ford slowing, limping on a front wheel as shreds of black rubber flew out from under the fender. I slowed and watched as Barron stopped the car, jumped out from behind the wheel. He didn't even look at the crippled car, just started sprinting in our direction. He had a chrome-plated pistol in his hand.

I goosed the Ram again, sped away toward the city streets.

"Does he honestly think he can catch us?" Liz asked.

"He just wants to get within range. He's thinking he can shoot out the tires."

"Can he?"

"He's not gonna get the chance."

The Ram bounced down a long slope toward civilization. I jumped a curb and hit the asphalt with squealing tires. At the top of the rise, I could see Bob Barron silhouetted against the blue sky. He'd stopped running, and he was waving his big paw in front of his face, trying to catch his breath in the dust I'd left behind.

I laughed out loud, a crazed cackle. But Liz Weston apparently wasn't one to enjoy the moment.

"What do we do now?"

"We get the hell out of Rio Rancho."

"But what about after that? We can't let those idiots wipe out the owls."

I hadn't been thinking about anything except escaping with my skin, but an idea popped into my head that made so much sense, was so simple, that I acted like I'd had it in mind all along.

"Don't worry. I've got a plan. There's somebody I want you to meet."

TWENTY-NINE

THE *GAZETTE* newsroom hummed with activity. Reporters clacked at computer keyboards, frowning, their neckties pulled loose. People clustered around beige desks, yakking and arguing. Others hurried around the huge open room on mysterious missions, their fists full of papers or photos or pencils. Phones rang and rang.

I watched the bustle through the glass wall that separated the newsroom from a small conference room Felicia had commandeered as soon as we'd shown up at her desk with our story of owls and bulldozers and murder. Felicia and Liz Weston hadn't taken long to get comfortable with each other. They stood at the round table, shoulder-to-shoulder over a map of the Rio Puerco, talking excitedly about the endangered birds and Tierra Verde.

I couldn't concentrate. What was I doing here? It had seemed like a good idea two hours ago, when my adrenaline was pumping from escaping bulky Bob Barron. What better place to hide out than a newsroom? What better way to protect the owls than through some publicity? What better ally than Felicia?

But now, I was nervous as a harelip in a soup-eating contest. Felicia was excited about the story, already had said more than once that it was destined for the front page. What would Tommy Greene think when he picked up tomorrow's newspaper? Wouldn't the publicity just put Felicia and Liz Weston into jeopardy? We couldn't hide in the newsroom forever. Eventually, we'd have to go home. More than likely, we'd find Bob Barron and his brutes waiting for us.

The owl photograph was proof David Field had known the colony was there, right in the way of the planned community. But that didn't prove Tommy Greene and his associates were the ones who had killed him. Before Liz Weston saw the photo, she'd been convinced Amber Field or one of David's girlfriends had done the deed. Who was to say that wasn't the case? We had no proof against Greene. Liz and Felicia might be able to stop the construction and save the birds, but they couldn't pin a murder on anybody.

That didn't seem to dampen their enthusiasm, but it played hell with mine. I wanted Tony the Tiger and his boys behind bars. Of course, the women didn't know what I knew: that Tommy Greene really was Tony Birbone, that he was accustomed to fitting people with concrete swimwear. I toyed with the idea of spilling it all, but I knew there'd be no persuading Felicia to keep it out of print. And that, for certain, would result in my untimely demise.

The phone on the table buzzed, and Felicia answered it.

"Great. I'll be right there," she said, and hung up. Then she turned to Liz and me.

"Sammy Flick just arrived. I'll go get him."

She scurried out the door, leaving me to explain to Liz that Flick was the spokesman for Tierra Verde. Liz moved around the table and sat across from me, leaving two empty chairs, facing each other, for Felicia and Sammy.

Sammy Flick's shiny head nearly twisted off his skinny neck when he spotted me watching through the wall of glass. He adjusted his thick glasses half a dozen times and swabbed his sweaty forehead with a white handkerchief before he reached his chair.

Felicia sat opposite him and made the introductions. When she spoke my name, Flick said, "We've met." He didn't look happy to see me.

I'd been impressed that Felicia could summon Flick to the newsroom with a phone call, without even telling him why she wanted to see him. Undoubtedly, this was part of why she loved her job. Not only can she sniff out the bad guys; she can make them dance to her tune. A newspaper, it seems, makes a pretty good hammer.

"What's this all about?" Flick asked.

Felicia didn't answer immediately. She just pulled the owl photo out from under the map on the table and handed it over. Flick looked at it, then tossed it back on the table a little too casually.

"It's a bird."

"Very good, Sammy," Felicia said. "Those correspondence courses are paying off."

"Cute. You dragged me all the way down here to look at a picture of a bird?"

"That's not just any bird, Sammy," she said. "That's an endangered species. And, after the paper hits the streets tomorrow, he's going to be a celebrity."

Flick pushed up his glasses, glanced at the photo.

"What's this have to do with me?"

"Guess where the photo was taken?"

"I have no idea." The bobbing of his Adam's apple suggested he had a very good idea.

"Right where you want to build Tierra Oeste."

"'S'at so? Well, that's too bad for the birds."

Liz Weston suddenly was on her feet, leaning over the table and barking into the face of the startled little man.

"No, it's too bad for you. An endangered species means a study and a halt to all construction. I think you people knew those owls were there all along and chose to ignore it.''

Flick looked ready to soil himself. A bronzed, brawny woman yelling in his face. A threat to construction of the planned community. A newspaper reporter who wanted to blare the whole business to the world. And maybe a private eye who wanted to pin a murder on his boss. Although, I must say, Sammy Flick didn't even seem to notice me anymore. The two women were challenge enough. Liz Weston towered over him, her weight on her splayed hands as she glared holes in his head.

Flick cleared his throat, pushed up his glasses, squirmed in his chair like a kid in the principal's office.

''We had wildlife experts check out that area before we ever developed the plans.''

''Oh?'' This from Liz. ''And how much were they paid to keep quiet?''

''See here—Miss Weston, was it?''

''*Dr.* Weston.''

''All right, Dr. Weston it is. You can get as worked up as you like, but it's not going to change anything. The construction won't be stopped, not in time to save those birds anyway. They can fly. They'll find another home.''

''No, they won't. They'll stay right where they are. I'll have my students out there lying down in front of the bulldozers before I let you destroy that colony.''

''Now, see here, that's not necessary. I'm sure we can reach some arrangement.''

''Yes, we can. You can halt construction immediately. Those birds are already in danger, just from the bulldozers shaking the ground.''

Felicia scribbled furiously in her notebook, getting down every word.

''The project won't be stopped,'' Flick said. ''Too much

money and too much planning have already gone into it. If you think you can stop progress by raising hell over some birds, you don't know New Mexico very well.''

Liz Weston seethed.

"I've lived here all my life. You might think you can pay off politicians or put pressure on the government planners, but I can pull strings, too.''

Flick's eyes, made big and flat by the thick lenses, blinked twice.

Stalemate. Maybe it was time for me to speak up.

"What about David Field?''

Flick didn't even glance my way.

"What about him?''

"He's the guy who took that photo. He knew about the owls. I'm guessing that's why he got killed.''

That got Flick to look at me. Other than the sheen on his face, he showed no reaction. Once the stakes climbed, he'd suddenly found his poker face. Maybe he thought this was one area where he could tell the truth; maybe he believed his company had nothing to do with Field's death. But he chose to play dumb rather than deny anything immediately.

"I don't have any idea what you mean.''

Felicia, after her unnatural silence, launched into him.

"What he means is, your boss is a suspect in the murder of David Field. Does that make it clear?''

Flick blinked, cleared his throat.

"Have the police made such a connection?''

"We haven't talked to them yet,'' Felicia said. "But I imagine they'll read all about it in the paper tomorrow.''

"I would be very surprised if your editors let you make such an allegation in print. They know, even if you don't, that such an unproven statement would be just cause for a libel suit.''

"You threatening me?"

"No threat intended. You do whatever it is you think is right. But I can assure you, Ms. Quattlebaum, that if you accuse Mr. Greene of murder, you'll be in court so fast, your head will spin. Good day."

Sammy Flick stood and left. He didn't even look back over his shoulder as he hurried for the exit. I could only imagine what he'd report to Tommy Greene.

"How'd I do?" Liz Weston asked Felicia.

"You were great, just great."

Liz smiled broadly. "It's all going into the newspaper?"

"Every word. By noon tomorrow, I'll bet we've got Fish and Wildlife officials crawling over every inch of that land."

"I hope you're right."

"Trust me. Now, you two go get yourselves a cup of coffee or something. I've got a deadline to meet."

Felicia sprinted out of the room, her notebook flapping.

Liz Weston turned to me, still beaming.

"We're going to stop them," she said.

"I hope so. I hope they don't try to stop us first."

The smile slid off her face.

"You worry too much."

"I saw what they did to David Field."

THIRTY

I HAD TROUBLE FALLING ASLEEP that night, too worried Tommy Greene or Bob Barron would burst in shooting, despite the chair I'd jammed under the doorknob. I'd persuaded Liz Weston to spend the night with friends, but Felicia and I wound up at our place, and the Terra Verde boys knew where we lived.

The anxiety gave me strange dreams. In one, David Field sat at the murder scene, untouched by bullets, clapping and flashing his brilliant smile while owls danced around him in a circle. He was like Dr. Doolittle, talking to the animals while they did the conga.

Later, I dreamed of Felicia. She and I sat in the window of one of the latte joints on Nob Hill, watching the traffic pass on the street outside while we sipped and chatted and smiled knowingly. What made the dream weird was that Felicia wore a sheer black negligee. We seemed totally unbothered by this wardrobe choice and no one stared—except me. Instead of feeling embarrassed because my sweetie's scrumptious bod was available to public view, I found myself bursting with love and desire. Perhaps that was the way my psyche wanted to see Felicia, warm and comfortable and happy to be with me—and mostly naked.

I hadn't seen that negligee in months. Felicia knew it was my favorite. Maybe she was saving it for our wedding night, the romantic honeymoon we planned to spend at a

Santa Fe hotel. Lord knows, we'd been too busy lately to work up to a night of candlelit romance. Between planning the wedding and making the world safe from Tommy Greene, we'd barely seen each other, much less made time for lingerie.

I awoke from the dream with a smile and a boner. It took me a second to focus after my eyes fluttered open. For an instant, I thought I must still be dreaming; then I knew what I saw was all too real.

Porkpie sat in the corner of my bedroom, looking very much at home. He perched on the narrow chair Felicia uses for dressing (and for an open-air closet, usually buried in clothes hurled in that direction). His dull black gun rested on his knee. Even scarier than the pistol was the fact he was reading the *Gazette*.

"Hey, Sleeping Beauty's finally wakin' up."

Too late to pretend I was still asleep. How long would he have let me languish there anyway?

"What are you doing here?"

He folded the newspaper neatly, turned it around so I could see the front page. Even from across the room, the bold headline was clear: CONSTRUCTION THREATENS RARE OWLS. A color photo showed the yellow bulldozers that had plowed a road through the empty desert.

"I thought I told you I didn't want a lot of attention focused on Tony the Tiger."

I sat up in the bed, pulled the covers up to my chest. My briefs were twisted in a knot, and I reached under the covers to untangle them. Porkpie's hand drifted to his pistol. I sneaked a peek at the clock, saw it was already past ten. Felicia must've gone to work before Porkpie slipped the lock.

"Yeah, well, see, I didn't want this to happen."

"Shaddup. I'm talkin' here. Let me read you somethin'."

He scanned the page, found the paragraph he was hunting.

"'Tierra Verde is owned by a mystery man named Tommy Greene. Company spokesmen won't reveal anything about Greene's background or his financial backers. No photographs of him are known to exist.'"

He glanced up from the page, his bad eye catching the light streaming in from the window.

"You think something like that ain't gonna get the attention of every bounty hunter in the country? That's like puttin' a big sign at Tierra Verde—TONY THE TARGET HERE."

"I don't see—"

"I said shaddup. I ought to just blow you away. You were warned not to mess in my business."

He waved the gun in my direction casually, just enough to remind me that one slip of the finger redecorates the room with my brains. They wouldn't fit into Felicia's color scheme.

"It wasn't me," I said quickly. "It was the women."

"What women?"

"My fiancée, the one who wrote the story, and that scientist, Liz Weston. I'm sure her name is in there."

"Yeah? The women put this together without your help? Why didn't you stop 'em?"

"You must not know women very well."

His mouth twitched, but he didn't allow himself to smile.

"So, nothin' you could do, huh? Not your fault?"

"Right. That's it exactly. But I kept my mouth shut about the other stuff. I didn't tell them about Greene's real identity or about the bounty."

"I can see that from the paper. If that had been in the article, you wouldn't be wakin' up today."

I swung my legs of the bed, keeping my hands in sight, keeping my privates covered with the comforter.

"Where you think you're goin'?"

"Nowhere, though it sure would be nice if you'd let me go to the bathroom."

"Don't move. I'm not done with you."

I'd figured as much. At least with my feet on the floor, I might be able to lunge at him if he decided to shoot. Better to go down fighting. I might get lucky. Maybe he'd shoot me only once or twice before I could wrest the gun away from him.

"See, the problem here is too much heat surrounds Tony the Tiger now. With this shit in the newspaper, the feds probably are swarming all over out there."

I shook my head.

"The birds are way out where they're building the subdivision. That's where the feds will be looking."

"Not those feds. I mean the ones who're supposed to protect Tony. They must know the news will get people like me lookin' out here in the sticks for him. Their security's probably tighter than Dick's hatband now."

I was thinking, That's probably just as well. This little man, despite all his tough-guy attitude, didn't stand a chance against Bob Barron and Greene's other bruisers. Maybe he'd forget the whole thing if he had to face a troop of federal marshals, too.

He must've read my mind. He leaned forward, fingering the pistol, not taking his eyes off me.

"I'm not quittin' now. I've come too far and invested too much not to collect that million bucks."

Stall.

"Maybe you'll have to wait until things cool off."

"No way, pal. I wait and every schmuck who thinks he can handle a gun will be swoopin' in here, tryin' to get my money."

"*Your* money, huh?"

"That's right. Mine. I got plans for that dough."

"Yeah? Like what?"

"Mind your own business."

"Looks like this has become my business."

He lifted a shoulder, half a shrug, as if he was thinking, What could it matter?

"I'm retirin'. Gonna open a legit business."

"Is that so? What are you going to sell?"

"What, you wanna horn in on that, too?"

"Just curious."

He thought it over a second.

"An escort service."

"Yeah. I thought you said legit."

"Hey, smart guy, that is legit. I'm no pimp. I'm talkin' classy broads here. They go out on dates with businessmen visitin' the city. But it's all on the up-and-up, see? No touchin' allowed."

"What if the girls decide to add a little hooking to their job description?"

"I don't think I'll have any trouble keepin' 'em in line."

Probably had a point there.

"What are you going to call this little operation? Escort services always have those cute names, right? Maybe you oughta call it Tony's Tigers, since his bounty money's paying for it."

"Oh, we are so fuckin' amusin', ain't we? If you must know, I'm callin' it Sonny's Honeys."

"That you? Sonny?"

"That's what they call me. My real name's Dante Campobello, but that seems like a mouthful for a business."

"Sonny's Honeys sounds better."

"Yeah."

He looked a little dreamy, as if he could see himself wearing fancy suits, arranging dates for lonely travelers.

"Well, Sonny, I'm sorry if I messed up your plans. But it was bound to happen, you know? Greene's making too many waves out there, throwing up this subdivision. Somebody was going to start paying attention."

"Yeah, it's just bad timin', that's all."

"Right, that's it exactly. Not my fault."

He squinted at me as if he had an idea. I was certain I wouldn't like it.

"What I need now," he said, "is somebody to distract Tony the Tiger and his boys. See, they're gonna be on guard now, and there's more of them than there is of me."

Sweat trickled down my ribs.

"Yeah, that's it. I need a...whatchamacallit, a *decoy*. I need somebody to get their attention while I come up behind 'em and pop Tony the Target."

I could feel my head shaking no of its own accord.

"Oh yeah. I need a decoy. And I think I know who that's gonna be."

"Look, Sonny, I'm not the kind of guy—"

"You better get dressed, pal. You don't want to go out to Tony's place in your underwear."

"I don't want to go there at all."

"That's too bad. I got a plan. And you're part of it."

He waved the pistol and my feet moved on their own. It didn't take me long to get ready, though I wasn't sure what a decoy should wear. I finally settled on jeans and sneakers and a blue polo shirt. Something I could move in comfortably. Shoes that would allow me to run like hell.

If I even had a chance to run. Going to Tommy Greene's meant it was a toss-up who'd shoot me first: Greene's thugs or Sonny Campobello.

You know what a decoy is, don't you? A sitting duck.

THIRTY-ONE

WE TOOK THE RAM, me driving and Sonny Campobello leaning against the passenger's side door, keeping his pistol trained on me. I tried to engage him in conversation, tried to get him to tell me his plan, but he was too busy pumping himself up.

As we entered Rio Rancho, he took stock of his weaponry. I could hardly drive for watching. He had the gun he kept pointed at me, loaded and chambered, the safety definitely not set. He had a matching 9-mm under his arm. He pulled up his pants leg to get a little five-shot revolver out of an ankle holster, flipped open the cylinder to make sure every chamber had a bullet in it. He dipped into a jacket pocket, produced one of those butterfly knives like you see in kung fu movies. He did some fancy twirling that made the six-inch blade appear, then fold back into the handles. Back into the pocket. He clucked his tongue, satisfied. My palms sweated so, I could barely hang on to the steering wheel.

We passed Tierra Verde headquarters, checked to see whether the big Buick Roadmaster was parked out back. Not there. Only a couple of cars parked in the lot, and I made them for belonging to flashy salesmen types. No standard-issue green Fords, no black-windowed land barge.

I drove on, then turned onto the road where Tony the Tiger had settled into his huge federally funded lair. Sonny told me to stop when we reached the hill overlooking the estate. Two green Fords and the Roadmaster were nosed in around the front door like horses around a trough. Sure looked like Tony was home.

"Okay, pal, here's what you do: You give me five minutes to get through this fuckin' desert out here; then you drive down the hill and park inside the gate. Just like you did last time, when they roughed you up."

"What's that supposed to accomplish?"

"Tony's protections will run out front to check you out. I'm goin' in the back."

"Then what?"

"Then I'm gonna pop that rat Tony Birbone."

"Won't they hear the shots?"

"Yeah? So?"

"Well, it'll be pretty clear I didn't fire them. They'll come after you."

"That'll be the last mistake they ever make."

"You're pretty confident."

"Bet your ass."

My ass definitely was on the line here. It wouldn't take J. Edgar Hoover to figure out I'd helped set up Tony the Tiger. Even if Sonny was successful, it was a sure bet Barron and the rest would come looking for me. I tried to express these concerns, but Sonny was already climbing down from the truck.

"Five minutes." He slammed the door before I could reply, and sprinted off into the scrub.

I watched the black suit and the gray hat until they disappeared from sight behind a sage-shaggy slope.

So here was my chance, right? Turn the truck around, haul ass. What could Sonny do about it? Oh, track me down, waste me with that arsenal of his, something like that. But at least running would buy me some time. I could go to the cops, tell all, get Erndow to give me some protection. Or I could get my own gun, currently safe in a drawer at home, and be ready to shoot it out when the bounty hunter came for me.

Yeah, right. Erndow would laugh me out of his office. He'd say he warned me to stay out his investigation. And he'd be right. And shoot it out? Who was I kidding? I didn't have the aim or, frankly, the guts to get into a firefight. Sonny Campobello looked as if he knew what he was doing, and nobody ever said that about me.

Then a third option occurred to me. I could play along. Sure. I'd drive right into Tony Birbone's estate, draw the attention of Bob Barron and the boys. Then, when the shooting started, they'd all run off after Sonny Campobello and I'd get the hell out of there. Might work. No reason for Sonny to come after me if I held up my end of the deal. And if it went badly for him, I could still run for the cops. Course, they might consider me an accessory. But better an accessory than a corpse.

I looked at my watch. Five minutes had passed, and I hadn't made a decision. I scanned Birbone's estate, caught a glimpse of a black suit disappearing around the back corner of the wall that surrounded the property. Shit. I couldn't let the little guy take on Birbone's goons by himself. Sure, he hadn't done anything but mock me and threaten me since we'd met, but I couldn't just leave him stranded. He was counting on me. I put the truck in gear, let it slowly roll down the hill, talking to myself the whole time: "Shit, shit, shit, shit, shit…"

The gate was open, and I drove right in like I knew what I was doing. This time, though, I stopped with the tailgate still outside the pillars that hid the electric gate. They weren't going to close it behind me twice.

I leaned on the Ram's horn, both to attract attention and

to let Sonny know I was in place. It worked on the first count. The front door of the house flung open and Bob Barron lumbered out from under the shade of the porch.

Guess he could see from there that I had the gate blocked. He didn't try that trick again. He just headed my way, charging like a bull. Hard on his heels came another muscle boy, one I hadn't seen before, one who had a shaved head and a neck thick as a telephone pole. He looked like a bullet in a suit.

Get out of the truck or stay inside? I opted to stay behind the wheel, but I turned off the ignition. As long as the motor was running, the temptation to flee was too strong.

They were on me in a flash. Bob Barron ran up to my side of the truck, and he wasn't even breathing hard from his forty-yard dash. Bullethead ran up to the passenger's side door. No getting out that way.

Barron didn't say a thing. He just crooked a finger to order me out of the truck.

It didn't seem possible that I'd forgotten how big the guy was in just twenty-four hours, but it surprised me when I stepped down out of the Ram. Looking up at his Frankenstein face could give a fellow a crick in the neck, not to mention bad aesthetic vibes. His shoulders were so broad, he could block out the sun.

"What the fuck do you want, you little shit?"

A fine greeting from someone who practically had bolts sticking out of his neck.

"I want to talk to Tommy Greene again."

"Again, you've got no appointment."

"I figured I'd park here until he agreed to see me. Nobody in or out."

The bruiser with the shaved head had slogged around to our side of the truck. He held out a hand the size of a pitchfork and said simply, "The keys."

I'd pocketed them. Now was the time to stall. If Sonny Campobello was shooting the place up, he certainly was being quiet about it.

"Uh-uh. Not until I see the boss."

Bullethead took a menacing step forward but he didn't get a chance to act. Barron stepped in front of him, effectively screening the brute from view, and reached for me. I tried to duck, but I wasn't quick enough, and he clamped onto my forehead with a thick hand.

Now, you'd think a man would have trouble squeezing a cranium as if it were a grape. Hell, most guys couldn't even reach around my bony head. But Barron got a grip on me like he was palming a basketball, and he squeezed— and squeezed.

I saw stars. Pain shot from one temple to the other like there was nothing in between to get in the way.

"The keys, shitheel." I could hear his voice, but all my brain registered was pain.

Desperation hit me, and I began to flail at the timberlike arm. My feet danced. I had to get free of his grip before my head popped like a balloon. He had me at arm's length and his arm was longer than mine. I couldn't reach him with fist or fingernail.

So I kicked him—hard. My aim seemed true, right between the legs, and something crunched in there. Barron's face didn't change expression. Did the man have no nerves, nothing to send a message of pain to whatever poor excuse for a brain resided behind those dead gray eyes? I kicked some more, alternating feet, my rubbery sneakers glancing off his shins and his knees. Something must've gotten through, because he suddenly let go of my head.

I had a pleasant split second, a moment of blessed relief, as the blood rushed back into my squished head. Then he back-handed my face so hard, I spun round and splayed out flat on the gravel driveway.

I wasn't unconscious—not yet anyway. I tasted coppery blood in my mouth. I felt big hands roughly digging into my pockets. I tried to roll over, to stall some more, but a foot came down squarely in the middle of my back and I was pinned there like a butterfly under glass.

My keys came free with a jangle and I thought with surprising calm, They're going to kill me now. They'll use my shiny new truck to drive my body out into the desert. It could be weeks before anybody finds me. Would anyone even care enough to hire Reed Hellstrom's helicopter to hunt for me? No one even knows I've come out here.

Then two loud pops echoed across the grounds of the estate. The foot came off my back, and I heard Bob Barron's rusty voice say, "What the hell? Get inside and see what that was."

Now's my chance, I thought. As soon as they go to investigate, I'll jump up, climb into the truck, and roar out of here. Only two problems with that plan: I wasn't sure which way was up, and they had my keys.

Then I felt a hand close on my bicep and I suddenly was on my feet. Bob Barron's face was inches from my own. His breath smelled of garlic.

"You're coming with me."

We took off across the broad lawn, Barron half-dragging me as he hurried toward the house. I needed my feet to function. I needed thoughts and reflexes and judgment. What I had instead was brain damage. I couldn't focus. I couldn't walk. If Barron had let go of my arm, I would've crumpled into a heap of useless protoplasm.

We reached the house, but Barron didn't drag me inside. He skirted the building, keeping as close to the wall as my limping form would allow.

My vision sharpened ever so slightly, and I saw he had a big Dirty Harry hogleg in his other hand. I let things go out of focus again.

When we got to the back corner of the white stucco monstrosity, he stopped, leaned me against the wall long enough to peek around at the backyard.

"Shit," he muttered. Then he grabbed me again, by the collar this time, and we went around the corner. He had me in front of him, using me as a shield, and I took comfort in the fact that Sonny, if he was any kind of marksman, could see plenty of places to shoot Barron without hitting me. It was like Oliver Hardy hiding behind Stan Laurel.

But there was no sign of Sonny. I blinked rapidly, as if sending semaphore signals, but no amount of clear vision turned up a black suit and a porkpie hat. Just the bulky redhead I'd seen at Tierra Verde. He wore a green Speedo and he floated facedown in the swimming pool, leaking red into the blue water.

Barron talked into my ear. "Who's back here? Who're you working for?"

"I don't know what you mean."

He twisted my collar so that it shrunk by several sizes. "Talk."

"Talk?" I squeaked. "I can't even breathe."

"Fuck it. Walk."

He pushed me forward and we moved toward the covered patio that shaded the back door of the house. The door stood open—I could see that much—but there was nobody around.

"Inside."

"Wait." I sounded like Mickey Mouse. "I'll talk."

"Too late."

He shoved me forward a few more steps. I didn't want

to go in that house. Gunshots would be flying, and I didn't want to catch a mistake.

Then Bullethead stumbled out the door, his arms held wide, as if he were happy to see us. He opened his mouth, and a gob of blood spurted out.

"Jesus." Barron was surprised enough that he lost concentration for a second, loosened his grip on my shirt. I took the opportunity to take a very deep breath. It was the best air I ever tasted.

Bullethead didn't make a sound. He turned very slowly, his arms still out to his sides, and twisted to the ground like a toppling crucifix. He landed facedown, showing off the hilt of the butterfly knife protruding from his muscular back, just above his shoulder blades.

"What the—"

Barron cinched me up tight again, pushed me through the door into the house. It was cool in there, dim and shadowy. A central hallway ran from the back door past several rooms and spilled into the great room at the front of the house. One of the doors opening into the hall was for the room where I'd slept off my beating last time I was here. Behind the others, who knew? But somewhere, Sonny Campobello waited to shoot this brute who breathed down my neck. And somewhere was Tony Birbone, dead or alive.

We edged down the hall, stopped when we reached a closed door.

"Open that door," Baron grunted in my ear.

I did not want to turn that doorknob. Who knew what was behind it? A Tiger? A bounty hunter? Barron twisted my collar, drove his concrete knuckles into the back of my neck. I winced, reached out, turned the knob.

I think my eyes were closed when it swung open, but when no shots rang out, I blinked them open. I saw an empty, tidy bedroom, as anonymous as the one where I'd lain unconscious.

"The next one."

Barron walked me across the hall to the next closed door, and we did it all over again. No one inside, but I recognized the phallic photo of the Empire State Building on the wall.

We zigzagged down the hallway like that, checking four doors without finding anyone. The house was quiet as a tomb. The fifth door, the one I remembered as being Birbone's office, was locked.

"Good," Barron murmured in my ear. "Now walk."

We marched toward the great room at the end of the hall, got to within ten feet of it before Sonny Campobello suddenly leapt into our path. He'd been hiding around a corner, and he was ready for us, his matching pistols at arm's length, the barrels pointed at Bob Barron's granite head.

Sonny hesitated, and I could see in his good eye that he was picking his shot, trying not to pop holes in his decoy. The bad eye worried me.

Sonny said, "Let the goober go."

Barron swung the hogleg past my shoulder, right next to my face, and his finger tightened on the trigger. I threw my arm up wildly, hitting his forearm and causing the shot to blast plaster from the ceiling. Then the air was full of explosions and whizzing lead and fire from the barrels of Sonny's pistols. Hot blood splattered my face, and I couldn't tell if it was mine or Barron's. All I wanted in the world was to lie on the floor and curl into a fetal position until I was either dead or safe.

Then I keeled over backward, dragged down by my collar as Barron fell. I landed on top of him with a thud and a squish and everything felt wet and sticky and wrong, wrong, wrong.

Sonny stood over me. He holstered one of his guns and tried to hoist me to my feet with one hand.

"You okay, pal?"

I wasn't sure. I took inventory of my body. Was any of this blood that spattered my clothes mine? I had pains all over from being slapped around by Bob Barron. My head felt like somebody had used it for batting practice. My neck felt like I'd just escaped a noose. I coughed and gagged. But there didn't seem to be any holes in me.

"You'll be all right," Sonny said. "I didn't hit ya."

He was right, though it took me another minute to be sure. Finally, I got up the nerve to turn and look at Bob Barron stretched out on the sopping carpet. His Boris Karloff face was pocked by three bullet holes, including one that had obliterated one of his colorless eyes. The other eye stared at the ceiling without seeing.

I tasted bile, was suddenly certain everything I'd eaten for the past week was coming up. But Sonny grabbed my elbow and wheeled me around, and I couldn't puke on him, not after he'd saved me.

"Have you seen Birbone?"

I shook my head, gestured backward without looking over my shoulder at Barron's body.

"We checked those rooms. All empty. His office is locked."

"Show me."

I shook my head. I'd had enough of the killing. But Sonny grasped my elbow, turned me back down the hall, and there I was, pointing at the office door.

Sonny stepped past the door and pressed his back against the wall. I did the same where I stood, so we framed the door like parentheses. Sonny checked the knob. Locked.

He looked up at me, flashed a smile.

"He's in there." Happy as an exterminator who's

trapped a rat, he winked the bad eye at me. My God, this man actually enjoyed this.

Then Sonny stepped away from the wall, pointed his pistol at the doorknob, and opened fire. Wood splintered away from the lock and Sonny kicked the door with his weight behind it and it swung open.

I didn't want to see what happened next. I didn't even want to be in this house. But something moved me to peek around the doorjamb as the little bounty hunter strode inside. Tony Birbone sat at his desk, writing with a yellow pencil on a pale green pad of paper. He looked up at Sonny as if he was surprised to be interrupted, as if he somehow hadn't heard the gunfire all around him.

Sonny trained his pistol on Birbone's face. I stepped into the doorway behind him, ready to try to talk him out of shooting. But Sonny was on a roll now.

"I've got a message for ya from Enrico—"

The desk exploded and smoke filled the room. Sonny Campobello slammed backward into my chest. I bounced off the opposite wall of the hallway. Then I was sitting on the floor, my back against the wall, my lap full of crumpled Campobello. Sonny's chest looked like hamburger.

What the hell? I tore my eyes away from Sonny, looked up through the cordite haze to see Birbone hoisting his polyestered bulk out of the high-backed leather chair. He held a sawed-off double-barreled shotgun in his left hand, the hand he'd had under the desk when Sonny burst into his office. The top of the desk bore a shock of splintered white wood where hot lead had erupted.

Birbone broke open the shotgun, pulled open a drawer, and produced two new shotgun shells, red plastic with bright brass rims. He pulled out the smoking shells and began to reload.

Holy Christ. I pushed Sonny to one side, tried to reach

his pistol, which lay on the bloody carpet six feet away. It was hard to scramble for the pistol and watch Tony Birbone casually reloading to finish me.

He snapped the abbreviated gun shut, then turned it toward me just as I got my hand on the hot barrel of Sonny's pistol. It was about to be over, all over, and Tony Birbone—mob rat, murderer, destroyer of owls—would walk away from it all. And I wouldn't.

Then, from far away, came the sound of a door crashing open.

"Freeze! Federal marshals!"

THIRTY-TWO

I TOLD MY STORY REPEATEDLY to the federal robots, pinning everything on the late Sonny Campobello. Hell, it *was* his fault I was there, wasn't it? I mean, I had a soft spot for the guy after he blasted Bob Barron off my back, but this was no time to be noble. The unsmiling feds wanted to put somebody behind bars here, and only Tony Birbone and I were left. They had an arrangement with Birbone. Me, they wanted to barbecue.

I found myself clinging emotionally to the marshals' boss, a guy with human attributes like normal posture and patience and the ability to smile. He'd shown up an hour into the interrogation, wearing a maroon sweat suit, Adidas running shoes, and a red baseball cap with a white *N* on the front. It didn't seem to bother him that his weekend had been interrupted by a bloodbath.

His name was Jim Tilley, and he'd told me he was a Nebraska native. He had the fresh-faced, corn-fed looks to prove it. He shooed away the Foster Grant types, sat me down in a back bedroom, and made his questioning seem less like an interrogation and more like a friendly chat with a guy who was, hey, just a little curious about how four stiffs ended up littering the hacienda.

After Tilley heard my story twice, he led me to the great room, past the bloodied hall, where evidence technicians in lab coats were picking up bits of brain and viscera with tweezers. The bodies had been wheeled away earlier, but I still felt queasy seeing all the spilled stuff that's supposed to stay inside of people.

Tony Birbone sat in a reclining chair in the center of the room, his feet up, looking pleased with the way armed feds in suits guarded every window and door.

Tilley gestured for me to pull up a chair, and he did likewise, and we sat facing the soles of Birbone's expensive loafers.

Tilley stroked his square chin, as if deciding how to begin. I sat quietly, but it was difficult. I wanted to stand and shake my finger in Birbone's cosmetically restructured face, to call him a killer and a thief and a bastard. But Tilly had instructed me to follow his lead, and I was doing what I was told, hoping I could trust the big, smiling Cornhusker to get me out of this without any prison time.

"Tony?" he ventured after a moment.

"Yeah? Jim! Hey, how are ya, pal? Long time no see." He acted as if he'd just noticed us sitting there, waiting for our audience with the big man. Fucker.

"Yeah, it's been awhile," Jim said. "No need for me to come visit as long as everything was going well. But now, I'm afraid your cover's blown."

Birbone rocked the recliner to an upright position, rested his elbows on his knees.

"I figured," he said. "Too bad, too. I was startin' to like it out here in the fuckin' desert."

"And you've been doing well," Tilley said, flashing his white teeth. "Built up quite a little empire."

Birbone threw out his hands in a gesture that said, Aw shucks, just doing what I can.

"We were willing to overlook the way you've funneled your mob holdings into this housing project," Tilley said, and the smile was gone. "We even looked the other way when you surrounded yourself with thugs like Robert Barron and when you used strong-arm tactics to increase your landholdings."

Birbone's eyebrows shot up and he opened his mouth to protest his innocence. Tilly held up a hand to stop him, let the smile dance around his lips some more.

"Don't bother, Tony," he said. "We've been watching you closely."

Birbone sat back, shrugged, as if thinking, What does it matter?

"But now, Mr. Mabry here thinks you killed a biologist named David Field, and we can't let that one slide."

Birbone shot me a look that said he was sorry he hadn't blasted me before the feds arrived. I was almost sorry, too. Death might've been a nice alternative to the splitting headache and assorted nicks and bruises that plagued me. And it might've saved me this whole song and dance with Tilley and the boys.

Birbone sucked a tooth, glanced around the room as if looking for an alibi. But then he gave that shrug again, the gesture of a man who was protected, who had nothing to lose.

"That was a mistake," he said. "I sent Bobby out there to watch Field, not waste him. We got our signals crossed."

I jumped to my feet.

"Come on! You had a man killed, and it's just a matter of 'signals' getting crossed?"

Tilley raised his hand again, calling a halt.

"Please sit down, Mr. Mabry. We'll get to the bottom of this."

I sat, stewing.

"Tell me more, Tony," Tilley said, his friendly voice

sounding like someone asking for the punch line to an old, familiar joke.

Once Tony Birbone finished making a show of glaring at my impudence, he turned back to Tilley and continued.

"Field came out to the office, wavin' around a picture of some damned bird. I told Sammy Flick to handle it, but the guy was makin' wild in the office, you know, so Sammy let him in to see me."

Birbone sighed, looked at his wristwatch, as if checking whether he still had time to fire Sammy Flick.

"So, Field comes in, tells me about this endangered species shit, says he can have the whole project shut down. I try to talk him out of it, see, and he says he's willin' to keep quiet for enough dough."

"You're telling us David Field *blackmailed* you? And you expect us to believe that? The man was a biologist. He really cared about—"

"Mr. Mabry," Tilley said again, shutting me down. He turned back to Birbone. "It does sound unlikely, Tony. The guy was a respected scientist."

"He was a scumbag. He said he wanted thirty thousand dollars up front to keep quiet about these fuckin' owls. He was all moony-eyed over some chippy named Monica and he wanted to skip the country with her. He wanted travelin' money. Then he had the balls to tell me he'd mail me his address so I could send him some more dough."

Uh-oh. The part about skipping with a dame was starting to sound like David Field. And Monica? Monica Gallegos? She'd said it was all over between her and Field, but maybe she'd lied. One thing was certain: If David Field was planning to run away with her, he'd need plenty of money— just to keep her in hair spray.

"So what did you do then?" Tilley asked.

"I told Bobby to follow him. That's all. But we only had a minute, see, because Bobby had to scoot out the door to keep up with the punk. I told him the guy tried a shake-down over some fuckin' birds and said Bobby should follow him and see where it leads."

Tilley tilted his cap back, rubbed his forehead. He looked like Birbone was making him tired.

"And then?"

"So Bobby comes back in a coupla hours and I say, 'Didn't I tell you to keep an eye on that guy?' and Bobby says, 'The guy's not goin' anywhere anymore.' What the fuck? I mean, that wasn't what I meant to happen, but Bobby had solved the problem, right? So I didn't chew his ass out too much. I let it slide. Guess I shouldn'ta done that, huh?"

Tilley shook his head slowly, as if his brain didn't want to accept what he was hearing.

"So you're saying Robert Barron killed David Field?"

"What, Jim? You're not listenin' to me?"

"Oh, I'm listening all right. It just seems awfully convenient to pin a murder on Barron after he's dead."

Birbone gave that easy shrug again. God, I wanted to slap him.

"I'm disappointed, Jim. I thought we had a relationship based on trust."

Tilley's face went tight for a second. When he spoke, the tone was low and certain.

"We have a relationship based on an agreement a federal prosecutor made with you. It's strictly business, Tony. Personally, I think you'd be a waste of good spit. But it's my job to hold up the government's end of the deal."

Birbone's eyebrows arched, but then he smiled. Bastard.

"I'm hurt, Jim, I really am. I thought we was pals. Oh,

well. I hafta tell ya, I was prepared for this moment. I knew you guys would try to welsh on me one of these days, and I thought it might be over this guy Field. I got somethin' to show ya."

Birbone rocked to his feet, strode off down the hall. With a look, Tilley sent one of the agents to follow.

Three minutes later, Birbone walked back into the room, carrying a plastic bag with a narrow gun inside. He handed it to Tilley, who grasped the bag carefully, staring in at the square pistol.

"That's your murder weapon," Birbone said smugly. "See, when Bobby came back and told me what he done, I made him hand it over. He didn't even have brains enough to ditch the fuckin' gun. I made him leave it on my desk, told him I'd take care of it. Then I put it in a bag and stashed it in my safe. Just in case."

Grudging admiration flashed through Tilley's eyes.

"You can prove any of that?"

"Check it out," Birbone said. "The gun's got nobody's fingerprints on it but Bobby's. The bullets will match the ones you took from the stiff."

"Why would Baron just hand over this kind of evidence?"

"Because I told him to. He was a good soldier. Also, I gave him a big shiny new pistol in trade. He liked it so much, he didn't question what I had in mind for the old gun."

A vision of Barron caressing the big hogleg like a kid with a Christmas toy danced through my head, and it had the stink of truth. Tilley seemed to feel the same way. He handed the bag over to one of his men, sat cracking his big knuckles for a minute, then turned back to Birbone.

"There's still the matter of Mr. Campobello."

"Hey, guy comes in here shootin'. I was protectin' my property."

"Yes, but he was here to collect a bounty placed on your head by Profundo. You've made too much noise in your new life, Tony. They're all going to track you down here."

Birbone grinned.

"Guess you guys gonna be pullin' some overtime, huh?"

"No, it's more serious than that. You're moving again, Tony."

"Aw, and things been goin' so well. I stand to make a killin' on this development deal."

"Killing is right," I muttered. "Killing off an endangered species."

"Hey, loudmouth, they're just fuckin' birds, okay? We can't let 'em stand in the way of progress."

"Looks like the birds win this round," I said. "If you're moving on, Tierra Oeste vanishes, right?"

"My investors ain't gonna drop this development just because I move on. We'll still be rakin' in dough off this deal when you're collectin' Social fuckin' Security."

What could I say? No doubt he was right. Given enough money, enough power, enough time, the developers always win—especially in a poor state like New Mexico.

I wanted to say more, but Tilley raised his peacemaker's hand again and told Birbone to pack a bag.

Minutes later, they were ready to go. I followed Birbone and Tilley outside, where the federal cars were parked haphazardly in the driveway. Someone had recovered my keys and pulled the Ram out of the way. I took some comfort in the way its fat tires had mauled Tony Birbone's lush lawn.

Agents began moving cars out of the way, pulling onto the street outside the walls.

"So where we headed?" Birbone asked Tilley.

"We're taking you to the airport. We've got a federal jet to carry you to a safe house until we get a new identity worked out."

"Another boring safe house. I hope you've got it stocked with liquor."

Tilley looked grim.

"I'm sure it has all your favorites."

I could hardly stand it. Guy's responsible for several deaths, his whole invented life wrecked, and he's worried whether they've got little umbrellas to put in his drinks. I couldn't believe he was walking away, that whatever deal he'd made with the feds was more important than the crimes he'd committed in the name of moneygrubbing Progress.

One of the marshals opened the back door of the Roadmaster for Birbone. I think it was the talker who visited me at Felicia's that day, but who could tell? They all looked alike. Birbone flipped Tilley a casual wave, climbed into the backseat.

The cars lined up in the long driveway, getting into position, a carload of marshals in front, the Roadmaster, another carload of gun-toting agents behind. Tilley and I stood on the front porch of Birbone's mansion and watched the cars move off, slow as a funeral procession.

I was turning to Tilley, my mouth open to complain, when a concussion hammered the air, orange flame lit Tilley's face, and I suddenly found myself flat on my back.

Shaking my head, I rose up on my elbows, to see the back of the Roadmaster was a flame-filled shell. The driver flung open the front door and staggered a few steps into the grass, his suit coat aflame, then fell on his face. Other agents sprinted toward him, rolled him in the grass to extinguish the fire. The entire trunk and backseat of the Road-master had been obliterated in the blast, along with Tony Birbone. Black smoke poured into the desert sky.

"Jesus, what happened?" I could barely hear my own words in my ringing ears.

Tilley, flattened beside me on the porch, took a moment to study the scene.

"Somebody just made a million dollars."

THIRTY-THREE

BY THE TIME THE MOP-UP was finished and Jim Tilley let me go, it was four o'clock in the afternoon. He'd questioned me more, naturally, asking me about the bomb, but I could tell his heart wasn't in it. Sonny Campobello certainly hadn't brought a bomb along when we drove to Birbone's hacienda. I would've noticed it in his arsenal. And the only thing I knew about bombs was that I didn't want to be anywhere in the vicinity of one.

I told Tilley I had to leave in time to make it to the tuxedo rental shop before it closed. Somehow, in all our earlier conversation, I hadn't mentioned I was getting married the next day. It made him smile, and he looked like he needed that.

Or maybe he smiled because I was such an unlikely-looking groom. Even after cleaning up in Birbone's gold-trimmed bathroom, I looked like hell warmed over. I still had the lump on my unshaven jaw. I had a red ring around my neck from Bob Barron twisting my collar around, and bruises on my temples where he'd tried to leave his fingerprints on my skull. My blue shirt was stained with other people's blood. My hair stuck out from my head like a tumbleweed. I reeked of gunpowder and sweat and fear and the smoke that once had been Tony Birbone.

Quite the pretty picture to present to José at the tux shop. The little twist came around the counter when the door tinkled me inside. He had his arms out in greeting, which made me think of Bullethead with the blade in his back. José got halfway across the sales floor, looking like he wanted to kiss me, before he froze.

"Mr. Mabry? What happened to you?"

"I've had a bad day."

José wrinkled his nose.

"*¿Qué peste?* Were you in a fire?"

"It's a long story. Can I just pick up my penguin suit and go? I'm tired."

José gave me a miffed look, then turned on his pointy shoe. Once behind the counter, he was no longer my new friend, but all business.

He found my paperwork, set it on the counter for me to sign. I didn't read it. For all I knew, it said I agreed to wear a tux every day for the rest of my life. I slid the papers back across the counter, and I found him staring at me.

"Is that blood on your shirt?"

I looked down at the brown stains, nodded.

"Oh my *God*. What happened?"

"I got my period." José winced in disgust. "You want to hand over the tux?"

He turned away, located the tuxedo among the others on the rack.

"Normally, we ask our customers to try them on before they leave the store. Make sure no mistakes have been made."

He gave me a once-over that took in the blood and the aroma and my lumpy face.

"I'm sure it'll be fine," I said.

José hesitated, unsure whether to trust the crisp white shirt and pressed black suit to someone who clearly was hard on his clothes.

"You'll get it back in one piece. I'm just getting married in it, not getting into any more shoot-outs."

José's jaw dropped, but he handed the tux across the counter. I snatched it away from him and strode out the door.

I'd pumped myself up into some sort of conquering hero by the time I got home, ready to tell Felicia how I'd survived the mob. She wasn't there.

The message light blinked on the answering machine, and I rewound the tape and listened to Felicia's voice: "Hi, hon, I'm calling to tell you I'm working late. There was some kind of shoot-out at Tommy Greene's home in Rio Rancho today, and they want me to write it for the front page. I'll probably be here into the night; then I'll pick up my parents at the airport and take them to their hotel. I'll see you when I get home. Love you. Bye."

I should've called her. I had the whole story she was chasing. But Tilley had told me to keep my mouth shut about Tony Birbone, and I was just flat too tired to tell it all again.

I hung up the tuxedo, poured myself a tall bourbon, and headed for the bathroom, stripping off clothes as I went. An hour later, I emerged, pink and pruney from a hot bath that washed away some of the trauma of the day. The speed with which the bourbon hit me reminded me I hadn't eaten all day, and I put on my bathrobe and shambled into the kitchen, feeling pleasantly fuzzy-headed, and made a sandwich.

By the time I finally got around to calling Felicia, she'd left the office. I pictured her at the airport, greeting her gray-haired parents as they got off the plane from Indianapolis, excitedly telling them about the wedding. It was a Kodak moment, a picture straight from Norman Rockwell, and it was the last thing on my mind before I fell asleep.

THIRTY-FOUR

I WOKE ON THE SOFA, sunlight streaming into my face. Felicia had thrown an afghan over me sometime during the night, but otherwise nothing had changed. In fact, I don't think I so much as twitched all night long. I creaked to a sitting position and found this note staring up at me from the coffee table:

> *Bubba:*
>   *I solved the David Field murder for you. You can congratulate me later. I've got to work this morning (bad form, I know, on one's wedding day), but I'll meet you at the chapel. I took my gown and makeup kit with me. I'm very excited the wedding's finally here. I love you.*
>
> *Felicia*

How's that for a kick in the pants? It shouldn't have surprised me, though. I've known all along I come second to Felicia's career. When she's on a hot story, I'm lucky if I can distract her long enough to get a hello. Still, it *was* our wedding day and we had preparations to make. I hadn't seen my bride-to-be in two days. A neat trick when you live under the same roof.

Beside the note lay the morning *Gazette,* its lead headline blaring above Felicia's byline: BLACKMAIL SCHEME BEHIND MURDER.

Jesus Christ, how does she do that? I snatched up the paper, skimmed the first few paragraphs. She had it nailed. David Field shaking down Tommy Greene and Tierra Verde over the endangered owls. Field getting smoked by the late Bob Barron. Barron dying in a mysterious shoot-out the day before at Greene's home. Greene's death by bombing. All of it, everything except Greene's secret identity and his connection to the mob—and the fact that I'd been present for the whole thing.

Much of the story was attributed to "sources," and I guessed the feds wouldn't say anything about it for the record. But Felicia had gotten it right, by and large, just by pumping the behind-the-scenes people she knew. It made me proud of her, but also proud of myself. Despite the superiority I sensed in her note—"solved the David Field murder for you" indeed—I knew I'd uncovered it all first by boldly following Sonny Campobello when I could've fled. Plus, I still knew some things Felicia didn't, like the mob connection, and I couldn't wait to tell her. What a wedding gift.

I called her office, but a secretary had no idea where Felicia might be.

Plenty of time for mob revelations later. I was getting married at eleven o'clock, and I should look my best, which wasn't easy, considering what I'd been through lately. I spent an hour in the bathroom, shaving and showering and grooming. I sucked down several cups of coffee, which made me jittery until I started splashing a dollop of bourbon into each cup. Jitters, I didn't need. My nerves were already shot, what with people shooting at me and people dying and bombs going off. What I needed was a long rest before embarking upon a life of wedded bliss. Our brief honeymoon in Santa Fe wouldn't be enough. I needed a vacation.

No time to think about that now. In a chapel across town, a caterer was putting out a huge luncheon spread and chilling champagne. Somewhere, a judge was readying his basso profundo to read the vows. At the Hilton, Felicia's parents were fussing over their clothes and corsages. Across the city, Felicia's workmates and my buddies were squeezing into their Sunday best to witness us getting hitched.

It wasn't a large affair, as weddings go, but a lot of people depended on me to show up and go through with it. My nervousness kept climbing and anxiety practically shrieked inside my head, but I fought the temptation to run for it. I owed it to all these people to put on the good show. And where would I go where Felicia couldn't find me? As many times as I've angered her over the past couple of years, I couldn't imagine how she'd react if I stiffed her on the Biggest Day of Her Life.

Between my fretful trembling and the booze, I could barely sort out how to dress in the tuxedo. The pants had little adjustable tabs on either side that I had to let out to accommodate those extra pounds I was carrying. The shirt had no buttons, just these little things that looked like cuff links that had to be inserted through the buttonholes. They came with instructions, but I kept dropping the little doodads, then crawling around on the bathroom floor to find them. The cummerbund was a challenge, and I wasn't sure which way was right side up. Finally, I decided the little pleats in the material should fold downward. Otherwise, they'd catch crumbs when you ate.

Every time I passed through the living room for more coffee, I glared at the phone. I needed to hear Felicia's voice, needed reassurance that the wedding would go off without a hitch, even though she was nowhere to be found. The phone just sat there, silent and smug.

Finally, I couldn't find any more reasons to hang around the apartment. I marched downstairs to the dusty Ram, fired it up, and drove to the chapel.

The chapel was a rental hall in back of a storefront along Central near Nob Hill. Felicia and I aren't religious people, so getting married in a church was out. I was nervous enough without some bleeding Jesus staring down at me the whole time. Felicia had located the hall, which was just a big room with blank tile floors and rusty windowsills. Though it was more suited to a business meeting or a family reunion, Felicia had started referring to the hall as "the chapel" in our planning sessions and I'd picked up that language. For weeks, that old song about "goin' to the chapel and we're gonna get married" had played in my head, until it had been replaced by "Tony, Tony, Birbone...."

Anyhow, I hadn't set foot in the chapel since we'd first settled on it as the wedding site, and I was surprised to find that somebody—Felicia, her friends, who knew—had decorated it with twisted crepe paper streamers and bouquets of flowers and a lectern for the judge to stand behind while we pronounced our vows.

I figured I'd be the first one there, but other people milled around already, straightening the rows of metal folding chairs and tasting the hors d''oeuvres and not looking nervous at all. I envied them. I felt like a wild animal caught in a trap. I didn't know whether to resign myself to my fate or start chewing off my leg.

Fortunately, my best man was already there, and I knew I could count on him to calm me down. It says something about me, I guess, that the person I settled on for best man is a cop—a homicide detective, in fact. It's not that Lt.

Steve Romero and I are so close. But most of the guys I know are shady characters who live along the Cruise. Romero was the only one I could trust not to hock the rings and disappear.

Romero's a large man with jet black hair and dark eyes and teeth white as a lighthouse. He's got an honest face, a sharp mind, and a cop's twisted sense of humor. Normally, our paths cross only a couple of times a year, more often than not in connection with one of my investigations. Romero has urged me for years to settle down with Felicia and get a real job, or at least get a better class of clientele. And he's very firm about discouraging me from messing around in police investigations. Fortunately, the David Field case had been bungled by the sheriff's department, not the APD, and Romero probably didn't even know how deeply I'd gotten entangled with murder and the mob.

"Hi, Bubba. You ready for the big day?"

I nodded and mumbled and twitched.

"Nervous? How can a guy like you be nervous? Guy brave enough to walk right into a trap at a mobster's house?"

I shushed him, took his thick arm in my hand, and led him toward a corner, away from the other guests.

"How do you know about that?"

Romero grinned. "I don't miss much. And everybody down at headquarters is talking about how you screwed up the feds' Witness Protection Program. You're a regular hero."

"Really?"

"Yeah, leave it to a screwup like you to give the feds one in the shorts. Cops love that shit."

So much for the "hero" stuff. I can always count on Romero to keep me grounded.

"Have you seen Felicia?" I asked.

"Nope. Nobody has."

"Shouldn't she be here by now?"

"She'll be here. The money was against you showing up, but here you are. Now, if you can just go through with it, I can make twenty bucks."

"You bet on the wedding?"

"Hey, your buddy over there was giving odds. I figured I could make a few bucks since I'm the one who's in charge of keeping you from running."

I looked past Romero's shoulder, toward where he had gestured with his thumb. Johnny the Hook was deep in conversation with somebody I didn't recognize, some schmuck that looked like a reporter. Johnny kept tapping the guy on the shoulder with his mechanical pincher to make his point. The half-pint reporter looked like it gave him the creeps, but he didn't move away. Johnny the Hook can be a commanding presence. He probably was trying to persuade the guy it wasn't too late to bet against me.

"I need a drink."

"Smells like you've already had a couple," Romero said, sniffing at me like a freaking bloodhound. "Want a mint?"

He rattled a box of Tic Tacs at me, held it out in offering.

"Any alcohol in those?"

He shook his head, grinning.

"Then keep 'em. I'll have champagne."

The caterer was an apple-cheeked woman with peach-tinted hair. She wore an orange orchid pinned to one shoulder strap of her apron and a name tag that said MRS. BEASLEY on the other. She looked on disapprovingly as I sloshed some bubbly into a stemmed plastic glass, but she didn't stare long. I probably scared her. With the tuxedo and my battered face, I looked like a cross between James Bond and Charles Manson.

Despite that, people kept wanting to greet me and offer their premature congratulations. I kept slugging down the champagne. Every time I looked at Romero, he rattled the Tic Tacs at me.

Felicia's parents, Roy and Doris, seemed determined to shake hands with everybody at the event. Considering that some were my pals from the Cruise, I hated to think what germs the Quattlebaums might be picking up. Roy, dressed in a gray suit that matched his Brylcreemed hair, had been into the champagne, too, and his Kiwanis Club smile seemed plastered on his face. Doris, sprightly in her floral chiffon, kept a hankie handy for tears that didn't come. At one point, they bracketed me and tried to kid me about stealing their daughter away, but the smiles froze on their faces when they saw I couldn't make a coherent response. Doris cocked an eyebrow toward the champagne, as if that explained everything, and she and Roy waltzed off across the room to shake Johnny's hook.

A big schoolroom clock hung on the wall, and I watched the minutes tick away. Still no Felicia. Even Romero was starting to worry. Johnny the Hook looked depressed, as if he should've been taking bets on her instead of me.

When a loud chirping went off behind me, I about jumped through the roof. The dumpy caterer twittered and said, ''Oh, that's me.''

While I puzzled over that statement, she located her Pullman-sized purse under the table, dug around in it for the tweeting phone, answered it.

''It's for you.'' She handed over a phone the size of a pack of cigarettes.

''Hello?''

''Mr. Mabry?'' The voice sounded distant, fuzzy.

''Yeah?''

''My name's Whitworth. I'm with the *Gazette*.''

Felicia's boss. Oh my God, what's happened to her?

"A photographer just brought me a message from Felicia. She said to call this number and tell you she's running late."

"Where is she?"

"Out where the environmentalists are demonstrating for the owls."

I sighed so heavily, I could hear it in the receiver, as if the gust of air had traveled through the phone lines to the *Gazette* newsroom and back again.

"We're supposed to be married in"—I checked the clock—"fifteen minutes."

"You know how she is."

"Do I ever. Thanks. Bye."

I handed the phone back to the caterer, who stowed it in her big handbag.

"Felicia's out on a story," I told Romero. "What should I do?"

"You want me to go get her?"

I glanced around the filling room. Some of the guests must've figured what was going on, because they were murmuring and nudging and glancing my way.

"You'd never find the place," I said. "I'll go. You, um, you make some kind of announcement, tell everybody to wait. Tell 'em to go ahead and eat, whatever. I'll be back quick as I can."

I walked on stiff legs out to the truck, muttering and cursing. How could she do this to me? Wasn't I terrified enough already? Why prolong my agony?

Then I was behind the wheel of the Ram, the champagne sloshing inside my head as I drove like a bat out of hell.

THIRTY-FIVE

I ROLLED UP TO A SCENE out of a Greenpeace brochure. Scruffy college kids and a few graybeards in shorts and Birkenstocks had linked arms, forming a ragged line across the desert. There were maybe thirty people out there, and I spotted Liz Weston's blond head bobbing in the middle of them as they faced down the enemy. A dusty yellow bulldozer roared at them, its toothed bucket upraised. The driver snapped the gears so the dozer lurched forward and stopped, lurched again. The machine resembled some prehistoric beast, eager to gobble up the protesters.

The demonstrators blocked the machine from the area where the owls squawked and fluttered around their colony of burrows. A handful of hard-hatted workers flanked the bulldozer, tools and survey stakes in their hands, looking ready to brain Weston and her gang rather than let them put a halt to the lucrative construction project.

Marching back and forth behind all this like a presiding general was my betrothed, Felicia Quattlebaum. Except generals rarely wear floor-length wedding gowns. Felicia jotted in her notebook, her eyes scanning the scene, oblivious to the Ram or to the fact the hem of her expensive gown was dragging in the dust.

The protesters shouted at the bulldozer and its minions, but whatever they were saying was drowned out by the rumble of the machine.

I needed this to stop. I needed Felicia to get in the truck and rush with me back to the makeshift altar in the rented hall. I needed to save face, to avoid looking like the jerk who got stood up because of some birds.

I flipped open the glove compartment, but my gun wasn't there. I'd left it at home. Hadn't expected to need it at a wedding, my own wedding.

I climbed down out of the Ram, trotted across the scrubland to where Felicia watched the scene unfolding.

"Bubba! What are you doing here?"

"What am *I* doing here? What are *you* doing here? In case you've forgotten, we're getting married right now."

"We are?"

She grabbed my arm, twisted it around so she could see my wristwatch. It hurt.

"Oh my God! I'm so sorry, Bubba. I'm not wearing a watch. The time got away from me."

"We've got to go."

"Not yet. Look, they're about to fight it out."

A couple of the construction workers ventured forward, prepared, it seemed, to knock heads until they'd cleared a path for the bulldozer.

"Oh shit." I moved to intervene, though how I expected to accomplish that, I don't know.

"Don't interfere!" Felicia shouted. "It's all part of my story."

"I can't let them whip up on my client and her friends."

"You can't very well fight them in your tuxedo."

I looked down at myself, what I was wearing, noticed the shiny patent leather shoes were already coated with dust.

"How about you? You're working in your wedding gown! Look at you. You're filthy."

Felicia seemed to have overlooked this. She examined

her gown where the dust had reddened it, saw that she'd ripped out part of the hem by walking on it. She looked up at me, shrugged.

"I changed in the car because I thought this would end soon and I could drive straight to the chapel. But the construction guys turned on the protesters. They know that if they can plow over those burrows, the owls will disappear and their jobs are safe. Liz and her people aren't budging. I couldn't walk away from bloodshed, could I?"

She beamed. I knew she wouldn't glow like this for me, even at the wedding. I threw up my hands, stalked away. Let her work. It's the thing she loves most.

Then I caught a flash out of the corner of my eye, and I turned, to see two cop cars barreling down the dirt road, their red and blue lights throwing color. They roared past the protesters' cars that lined the dusty road, bounced into the scrub, and stopped directly in front of the bulldozer.

Lieutenant Erndow stepped out from behind the wheel of the first car, straightened to his usual erect posture, and held up one hand toward the bulldozer, as if he could stop it with a simple gesture.

It worked. The bulldozer driver shut off the engine, and a sudden silence swallowed up the desert.

A guy with blond muttonchops and a khaki shirt climbed out of the other side of the patrol car. He waved a sheaf of papers over his head like a white flag.

Felicia trotted toward Erndow, her white gown flapping, and I followed. I'd never get her to the wedding if she got herself arrested.

Felicia and I joined Liz Weston and the bulky bulldozer driver in a clump around Erndow and the guy in khaki, who turned out to be Stan Jones, the eulogist from David Field's funeral. The protesters and the construction workers hung back, watching the four deputies who'd piled out of the second patrol car. The deputies stood with their hands on the butts of their pistols, daring anybody to make a wrong move.

Erndow's eyes raked my tux, then went to Felicia in her gown.

"You two fall off a wedding cake?"

Oh ho, humor from Old Ironhead. Liz Weston grinned. I felt like stomping their toes with my once-shiny shoes.

Felicia introduced herself and Liz to Erndow, who in turn introduced Jones, saying he represented the U.S. Fish and Wildlife Service. Jones cleared his throat and held up the papers for us all to see.

"This is a cease and desist order," he announced in a cracked voice. "We're calling a halt to all construction until a study can be done on the Mexican owls out here."

A cheer went up from the protesters. Liz Weston clenched me in a big hug. More wrinkles to my tux.

The construction workers glared, but Erndow gave them a stern look that sent them scurrying toward their pickup trucks.

Felicia closed in on Jones, firing questions about the specifics of the order.

"Excuse me, Lieutenant," I said as I squeezed past Erndow.

I grabbed Felicia's arm and led her away. She shouted to Jones that she'd call him later for details, then allowed herself to be dragged to the Ram.

The last thing I saw before I turned toward the truck was Liz Weston standing and watching us, her fists on her hips, her white teeth glowing on her brown face. A happy client. What a rare and wonderful sight. I'd begun to think *they* were an endangered species.

THIRTY-SIX

FELICIA APOLOGIZED SIX TIMES on our way to the chapel. Somehow, the apologies would've seemed more heartfelt if she hadn't been brushing her hair and dabbing on makeup the whole time, studying herself in the rearview mirror she'd twisted toward her without even asking first. Telling me she was sorry seemed like just one more of the duties she needed to accomplish quickly before we reached whatever remained of our wedding.

I gave her no reply, hoping the silent treatment would communicate just how angry and frustrated I'd become. She didn't seem to notice, too busy chattering about Liz Weston and bulldozers and last-minute rescues by the cops. Finally, I could stand it no longer.

"Damn it, Felicia, we're supposed to be getting married right now!"

She snapped shut her compact and squinted at me.

"And we will. Everything's going to be fine."

"I'll be surprised if anybody's still there."

She smiled.

"They'll be there. They've got to see how it all turns out. I'll bet the suspense is killing 'em."

I was thinking, It's killing me, that's for sure. My stomach gurgled and my hands shook and the champagne had given me a headache.

"Besides," she said impishly, "my mother wouldn't let

anybody leave. She's probably thrown herself across the doorway.''

We landed in the parking lot in a squeal of rubber and slamming doors. Romero stood outside the door of the hall, pointedly looking at his watch.

"Yeah, yeah, I know. We're here. Finally."

Felicia burst right into the hall, her skirt gathered in one hand, her composure as complete as if she'd been waiting outside the chapel the whole time. Maybe nobody would notice her hem was ragged and dusty.

The open door let out a keening squawk of organ music, which changed to a *wack-a-wack-a* funky beat. A deep voice rolled out the door behind it, singing about how ''my baby put me down.''

I could've done without the singing, not to mention the sentiment.

"Where'd you get the guy on the organ?" Romero asked.

"You don't know him? That's Willie 'Porkrind' Jefferson. He's an old bluesman. Famous down on the Cruise."

"He's put on an unforgettable performance for your wedding guests. Got people to dancing. You should see Felicia's parents. Those Arthur Murray lessons sure pay off."

Felicia had left the music to me, the one thing I'd arranged solo, and I'd picked Porkrind to play the wedding march. Who knew he'd have an hour to wallop the guests with his version of the Motown sound?

Romero grinned at me, waiting. I didn't let him down.

"Let's do it."

"Attaboy."

Porkrind abruptly cut off his wailing when he saw me come through the door. He'd worked up a sweat, pumping out his funky stomp, but he wiped his shiny forehead with a handkerchief and settled into the pomp-pomp he'd been hired to play.

I noticed as Felicia took my arm that the buffet had already been trashed. Dirty paper plates perched precariously on every flat surface. Plastic forks littered the floor. At least the crowd hadn't gone hungry. As we marched along past familiar faces, it looked like most of them had been into the champagne already, too. Or maybe they were just flushed from Porkrind's performance.

I was grateful the white-haired judge had stuck around for our return. As soon as we arrange ourselves in front of him, he looked down at a little black book and opened his mouth to intone the vows.

I had trouble following the ceremony. My mind whirled with all the abandonments of my life: Norton and Junior walking me into the woods. My dad climbing into his Kenworth. All the old girlfriends and clients who'd decided I wasn't cutting the mustard.

What was I getting myself into? I'd constructed a life free of long-term commitments and their resulting disappointments. Nothing hurts you if nothing matters. Now, with this ceremony, I was casting aside all that caution. I was saying, in public, that Felicia was the only woman for me and that I promised to be true. More importantly, I was saying I trusted her never to leave me.

Felicia squeezed my hand to signal me when it was time for me to say "I do." It came out a croak, but I got it said.

Romero handed over the rings. I managed to slide the slim gold band onto Felicia's hand without dropping it, and the judge said, "You may kiss the bride."

Then I was lost in the kiss, oblivious to the crowd, my misgivings forgotten.

When we finally came up for air, the crowd was laughing and cheering. A warm blush spread over my face, making my pals laugh even harder. I didn't care. I was past embarrassment now. I'd survived the wedding ceremony. Of all the dangers and humiliations I'd faced recently, this was the one I'd feared the most.

The revelers had managed to stay out of the wedding cake during the party that preceded our nuptials. In a daze, I followed Felicia over to the three-tiered confection. The worst was over. The rest was a party.

Porkrind Jefferson pumped away at the keyboard while Doris hugged Felicia and Roy pounded me on the back. Doris's eyes were filled with tears of joy and Roy looked as if he'd just won the lottery. We switched partners for more hugs all around. Then the Quattlebaums made way so Felicia could cut a fat slice of the sticky cake. She stuffed it into my face with a little more gusto than I thought necessary, but what the hell, we were celebrating.

Doris passed out portions of the cake while Felicia and I stood against the wall, accepting congratulations and basking in the moment.

I may have been wrong about Felicia. I'd thought nothing made her happier than doing her job, exposing the bad guys. But I'd never seen her glow like this. I made another of those silent vows to myself. I'd try to make her this happy every day of our lives together.

By the time we'd shaken all the hands and kissed all the proffered cheeks, most of the crowd had trundled outside with their handfuls of rice to hurl at us.

People hooted and cheered when we ran through the door into the bright sunshine. I had my head down to keep the rice out of my eyes and my hand on Felicia's arm as we sprinted for the truck. Suddenly, Felicia pulled up, and I nearly fell over backward from the quick stop.

"Wha—"

Amber Field stood next to the Ram, glaring at us. An

incongruous thought: We didn't invite her to the wedding. Then I saw the pistol in her fist, pointed at my midsection.

"Hey! What are you doing?" I couldn't keep the indignation out of my voice. Hadn't I had enough trouble for one day? Hadn't our wedding nearly been ruined already because of those damned owls? What did Amber Field want? And did we have to discuss it right then?

Then I saw something that chilled me as much as the pistol. In her other hand, Amber held a copy of the morning *Gazette,* its headlines blaring about her late husband's infidelity and attempted extortion.

Amber's eyes looked as if something were on fire in her head. Something had snapped inside her, and it had led her here, to our wedding, with a pistol in her hand.

"What's this about?" Felicia demanded.

"You," Amber said. "You two are responsible for this."

She shook the newspaper at us like we were bad puppies.

"You've ruined my husband's good name."

"Hey, lady," Felicia said, and I wished so badly that she would shut up, "we didn't do it. He did it to himself when he tried to blackmail Tommy Greene."

"Lies! All lies! David was perfect in every way. He'd never do such a thing. He'd never abandon me."

I caught movement at the corner of my eye. I glanced over, to see Romero moving at a crouch to sneak up on Amber Field. Only my giant truck stood between him and a rescue. I didn't know how he expected to get to her without somebody getting shot first. Probably me, since that's where the gun was pointing.

Amber Field's white Nissan was parked behind the Ram, and maybe Romero could slip between the two vehicles and—

Hey, wait a minute. That little white car. I looked again

at the pistol in Amber Field's trembling hand. Looked like a .22. She was the one who fired the shots at me in the parking lot outside Felicia's apartment! She was the one who tried to scare me away from the case. No wonder she'd fired me the next day. She'd tried to remove me altogether. Why? Just because I was getting close to revealing that she'd married a scumbag?

The sudden knowledge left me cold. I had to do something, and quick. Felicia, in her usual bulldog manner, was trying to talk Amber Field into handing over the gun, or at least getting out of the way so we could finish our wedding departure. But I knew now that Amber's pistol wasn't a bluff. She was willing to use it, had used it before, and we were much easier targets this time, standing only six feet away.

Amber turned the gun on Felicia, ready to silence her insistent blather, and Felicia did something so unexpected, it's a wonder I wasn't just struck blind and turned to stone where I stood. She threw her bouquet at Amber's face. The flowers smacked Amber dead-on, and I lunged at her, reaching for the gun.

Crack!

The gun recoiled in her hand as I wrestled her for it. Then I had her on the ground, my weight on top of her, both hands gripping her wrist. She grasped the gun tightly, but then a big brown hand came into view and deftly snatched it from her. I looked up. Romero stood there, the gun safely held out of reach over his head. He was looking past me. I turned to see, and I found a clump of people tightening around Felicia. Through their legs, I saw a splash of red on her white gown.

I jumped off Amber Field and pushed people out of the way to reach my new wife.

She lay on her back on the asphalt, her face twisted, her

right hand gripping her left shoulder, where the gown was soaking up blood.

I crouched beside her, cradled her head against my knee. The bullet had gone cleanly through her shoulder, and I felt blood seep out of her back and into my tuxedo pants.

"Sweetie? Can you hear me?"

Felicia's eyes fluttered open. The sight of my worried face made her smile a little.

"Did you get the gun away from that bitch?" she asked, and I knew then that she would be okay.

"Yeah, I got it. Romero's sitting on her."

"Good."

She closed her eyes, grimaced against the pain. Somewhere in the distance, an ambulance siren wailed. She looked up at me again, a grin tugging at the corners of her mouth.

"You hear that?" she asked, and I nodded gravely. "They're playing our song."

EPILOGUE

THEY MADE ME PAY FOR the tuxedo. The folks at the dry cleaners got the blood out, but José was pissed, and he charged me full price anyway. Now I have a fancy-pants suit hanging in my closet. I hope I never have another occasion to wear it.

By all accounts, we made a haul in wedding presents. I vaguely remember noticing a table stacked high with gifts in the chapel. But we never received them. After the shooting, while everyone was busy with the ambulance and the cops, someone (probably one of my so-called friends) made off with all the loot through a side door. Sure made it tough to write those thank-you notes.

Felicia and I spent our honeymoon at the hospital. It took her a couple of months to recover full motion in her shoulder. She's predictably perverse about the puckered round scars the bullet left behind. She's taken to wearing wide-necked blouses that fall off her shoulder and expose the scars to public view. She says they make a nice conversation piece. I suggested she get a biker-mama tattoo on the other shoulder and start wearing halter tops. Then she'd never be at a loss for conversation. As if she ever is anyway.

Amber Field, last we heard, was improving at a residential clinic for people with mental problems. A judge sent her to the clinic after ruling her unfit for trial. There was some question about intent anyway, and though I resented the implication that Felicia wouldn't have been shot if I hadn't gone for the gun, I didn't feel inclined to insist on jail time for David Field's widow.

Amber told the court psychiatrist that she'd spotted me talking to Monica Gallegos that day at UNM. She'd gone to the university, gun in her purse, to threaten the people who were spreading rumors about her beloved David. When she saw me talking to Monica outside the Biology Department, something cracked inside her. She followed me back to Felicia's apartment and tried to shoot me in the parking lot. I still don't know why her madness turned her on me, but I've accepted that grief can shake loose a person's moral grounding.

Monica Gallegos testified at Amber's hearing, testily admitting that she and David Field had planned to run off together. I'll never understand what made Field want to throw his life away on someone as shallow as Monica, but Doc Slagg, who sat next to me at the hearing, ventured that Field had finally met his carnal match. Monica, apparently, had appetites as powerful as his own and abilities to match. Or, as Slagg put it, "I hear she can suck the chrome off a trailer hitch."

Liz Weston saved her owls. After the revelations about Tony Birbone and the mob made the papers (under Felicia's byline, of course), Tierra Verde's financing evaporated. Somebody may build a whole new town out in those boonies one of these days, but the owls will be protected.

Far as I know, the feds haven't figured out who planted the bomb in Tony Birbone's car. Whoever picked up a million bucks by turning Birbone into individual molecules must be lying low, counting his dough. Maybe he'll use it to start a business, just as Sonny Campobello had planned to do. Though I doubt New York needs another escort service.

Through Felicia's crusading, Harry Whitewoman got his land back, along with his good name. A judge ruled Whitewoman had been strong-armed into signing away the deed, and he voided the sale. Nobody from Tierra Verde showed up to contest the decision.

Speaking of deeds, Felicia and I have become home owners. She couldn't just lie around while she was recuperating, so she poured all her energy into finding a house we could afford. As usual, I went along for the ride, nodding and signing whatever Felicia told me to. Hell, she's the breadwinner; let her pick which house she wants to make the payments on. She did well, with the help of a real estate agent who was the sister of Denise at the bridal registry. That family's got a lock on people starting new lives together.

The house is a little brick charmer not far from the university, close enough to the Cruise that I can go for a beer with my pals without driving across town. The house isn't much bigger than the apartment we left behind, but it does have a spare bedroom with its own exterior entrance, which we've converted into an office for me. First time in my life I've had my own office. I've got a secondhand desk, my own phone, everything. A tasteful brass plaque hanging on the wall outside the door reads: BUBBA MABRY, PRIVATE INVESTIGATIONS. My shingle. Open and ready for business.

On the wall above the desk, right where I can see it when I'm on the phone trying to drum up clients, hangs a framed photograph. It shows an owl with yellow eyes, a compact body, rangy legs. The bird looks down on me with an expression that mixes ferocity and disdain. On good days, I like to think I can detect a little gratitude in that glare.

FRIENDS AND ENEMIES

A MELLINGHAM MYSTERY

SUSAN OLEKSIW

Preparations for the twenty-five-year reunion for graduates of Mellingham High School are under way—and trouble tops the guest list. Becka Chase has her hands full between preparations and fending off the advances of her neighbor and ex-lover.

Eliot Keogh has returned to find out who framed his father and sent him to prison. Becka's neighbor Mindy has run off without a trace. Her husband, Vic, is found in a coma. Police chief Joe Silva's razor-sharp instincts zero in on the kind of mystery that can happen only in a small picturesque town where friends and enemies can be one and the same.

Available May 2003 at your favorite retail outlet.

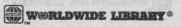

WORLDWIDE LIBRARY ®

WWMF&E

IN
AND
OUT

A DON PACKHAM AND
FRANK MITCHELL MYSTERY

Mat
Coward

Whether he's miserably depressed or buoyantly
cheerful, a day with the delightfully unpredictable
Detective Inspector Don Packham is never dull
for his partner, DC Frank Mitchell. When the body
of Yvonne "Chalkie" Wood, a member of
the Hollow Head Pub's darts team, is found
bludgeoned, Packham and Mitchell accept
an unspoken challenge from a clever killer.

Her untimely murder puts the detectives on
a case of money, sex and secrets that requires
luck, skill—and an excellent aim—to solve.

Available May 2003
at your favorite retail outlet.

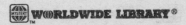

WWMI&0

STOLEN HONEY

A RUTH WILLMARTH MYSTERY

NANCY MEANS WRIGHT

When a local university student is found dead in
a patch of deadly nightshade, Gwen Woodleaf turns
to neighbor Ruth Willmarth for help. The dead young
man had driven Gwen's mixed-race daughter,
Donna, home from a party, and suspicion points
to both Donna's overprotective father and
a farmhand with an unrequited crush on the girl.

Donna's brutal murder leads Ruth to a shattering
revelation about some of Branbury's oldest families,
and to the discovery that hatred here runs
deep enough to kill.

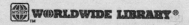

"...penetrating, economical,
and generously plotted..."
—*Kirkus Reviews*

Available April 2003 at your favorite retail outlet.

DEADLY MORSELS
The table is set for murder...

TAKIS & JUDY IAKOVOU
STEVEN F. HAVILL
JANE RUBINO
PETER ABRESCH

ANOTHER'S CURSE Takis and Judy Iakovou
Could things get any worse for the Oracle Café owners Nick and Julia Lambros when rats appear in the Dumpster and moonshine turns up in the lettuce crates? Unfortunately, yes—when the health inspector who shuts them down is found dead!

RED OR GREEN? Steven F. Havill
When Posadas County, New Mexico sheriff Bill Gastner finds his oldest friend dead of an apparent heart attack, something doesn't ring true. It turns out that George succumbed to a poisoned Burrito Grande, and it takes the well-seasoned Gastner to find out *who done it.*

CAKE JOB Jane Rubino
Cat Austen is covering a lush bridal expo in Atlantic City, helping her future sister-in-law pick out a wedding cake. She soon finds herself in the middle of a major mafia shakedown involving pastry chef Patty Cake and a hired killer known as "El Cocinero."

SHEEP IN WOLF'S CLOTHING Peter Abresch
Jim Dandy and Dodee Swisher head for North Carolina's scenic shores for a weekend Elderhostel on culinary magic. When the surf washes up the body of a local priest, Jim and Dodee follow a trail of murder most fishy—and end up in dangerously deep waters....

Available April 2003 at your favorite retail outlet.

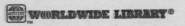

WORLDWIDE LIBRARY ®

WWMDM